Alien Cure

Jerry Steen

Published by Jerry Steen, 2022.

This is a work of fiction. Similarities to real people, places, or events are entirely coincidental.

ALIEN CURE

First edition. June 13, 2022.

Copyright © 2022 Jerry Steen.

ISBN: 979-8201539214

Written by Jerry Steen.

Table of Contents

Chapter 1 The Day of Apocalypse ... Almost

I will never forget that day: The Day of the Apocalypse. The day when Mutual Assured Destruction was considered a viable choice for our leaders.

I thought that 9-11 was a big day. OK, it was a big day, but not compared to the day that the full-scale use of high yielding weapons of mass destruction became a reality. It was the day that we were told would never happen because our world leaders believed in the theory of deterrence. On top of that, who wants to be the president that "pushed the button?" It was expected to be stable global peace, with its share of tension between countries. It worked for nearly a century.

The sight of the bright light from nuclear weapons being blasted over some of our major cities was a shocking experience. I just knew that things would never be the same. Just like 9-11 left our country changed forever, I knew these blasts would reshape our country.

The sight of seeing our ICBM's blasting off from our bunkers in our remote locations in Montana, North Dakota, and Wyoming made my blood run cold. To know that those missiles, launched from my country, were going to create indescribable damage on other countries quaked me to the core. The sight of seeing other countries' weapons reach our shores caused me to shake in my shoes. I dropped to my knees as I saw these missiles on a collision course for my country.

As these missiles disappeared into nowhere, I was full of wonder and amazement. I thought, "How in the world did this happen? Who delivered our country? Who saved our world?"

As much as I wanted the answer to these questions, I wish I had never found the answer. It tore apart our family. It tested my survival skills while I was on the run. Most of all, it tested my faith as nothing ever has. Not long ago, I was enjoying life as it was. The way it was "supposed to be". The way of life I would love to return to, but never will see again. Let's go back to where it all started just a few months ago...

Chapter 2 At the Crusade Tuesday Night

I never really thought too much about end times until Dr. Card came to the Bible Baptist Church. David Birch had invited me to hear him teach about the second coming of Christ—repeatedly. He was excited about Dr. Eugene Card coming to his church and was inviting everyone at work as well as his neighborhood to hear Dr. Card's teaching. David had bought all his books, tapes, and videos. He even let me borrow one of his books to read. I never did read it. In fact, it was still in my bookshelf when Dr. Card came to town. Of course, I had to go the first night, or I would pay for it the next day at work when I saw David.

After opening prayer that Tuesday night when the first meeting began, David took the stage with the rest of the Sojourner Quartet. David has one of those real deep voices that I always wish I had. He can sing bass as well as anyone. He had a portly body that went well with his deep voice.

Frank Fuller was the lead singer. He was rather tall and thin. He sang in a country band until he committed his life to Jesus Christ at the Bible Baptist Church about five years earlier. You can still see the effects of his lifestyle on his wrinkled face. Now he is using his voice to glorify God. I thank God for His patience, mercy, and forgiveness every time I see Frank. They were singing an old song called "Midnight Cry". Frank's face was glowing as he sang the difficult chorus line. I could tell the song touched many hearts because of the tears I saw on the faces of those around me. I couldn't help but think of how glorious it will be when Jesus returns and I will see Him face to face.

After the quartet finished and the shouts of glory and applause died down, the local pastor, Reverend Paul, stood and began his introduction of the speaker. "I want to welcome all the visitors here tonight. I also want to announce that there is plenty of good food following the service in our fellowship hall after the meeting in our fellowship hall. Just follow the quartet as they run to the hall with fork in hand." The crowd laughed as the each of the quartet holds up a fork. "You thought I was kidding, didn't you?" Pastor Paul said.

"I encourage every person here to join us every night of this End Times Crusade. Our guest will be sharing a series of events that may not be too far down the road. He will put the pieces of the puzzle together into a tightly woven fabric of events that will be, as our guest puts it, 'as clear as today's newspaper'. I had heard this man a few years ago. He reminds me of a professor back when I was in seminary. He has so much information to impart and I know he could teach for three weeks about Jesus' second coming and just scratch the surface. However, we only have him for six days, so I want to turn the remainder of the service over to him. My friends, I am pleased to introduce to you author and teacher, Dr. Eugene P. Card." The applause was loud as Dr. Card took the stage. The people in the congregation were visibly excited. They quieted as the speaker raised his hands. Dr. Card was a very small man. As he began to speak, I could hear his crisp, clear voice as he precisely wove his story.

"Thank you for your kind remarks, pastor, and thank you for your hospitality. I surely feel welcomed here and hope you feel as comfortable with me as I do with you. I also am ready to dig into that good food I saw coming into the fellowship hall earlier. However, I did not bring my own fork." The audience laughed.

"You see behind me a chart," as Dr. Card pointed behind him, "This chart is a visual guide through the end time events that I will be sharing with you. You will find a smaller version of this for sale in the foyer also."

"First, let's get an overview of end time events. This will give you a snapshot of future events." Dr. Card says as he turns toward his event chart. "At the top, you can see the major events that will happen—the Pre-tribulation Rapture of the Church, the 7 Year Tribulation Period, the Millennium, and the final major event, the New Heavens and Earth. As you can see, there are many events that take place during these major events."

"The 7 years of tribulation is the period of time when the Anti-Christ will rule the Earth. The Millennium is the thousand-year reign of Jesus Christ. The New Heavens and Earth is the time when all tears will be wiped away and God's Kingdom will be set up forever."

"Tonight, we will focus on the first event that will set all other events into motion, the pre-tribulation rapture of the church. Now, if you do a word search on your bible software or look in an exhaustive concordance for the word 'rapture', you will come up empty because this word in the English Bible will not be found in scripture. However, the event is described in the bible as clear as can be."

"Turn in your bibles to Revelation Chapter four. In verses one through three, you will see a description of this wonderful event. Please read along with me."

"'After this I looked, and, behold, a door was opened in heaven: and the first voice which I heard was as it were of a trumpet talking with me; which said, Come up hither, and I will show thee things which must be hereafter. And immediately I was in the spirit: and, behold, a throne was set in heaven, and one sat on the throne. And he that sat was to look upon like a jasper and a sardine stone: and there was a rainbow round about the throne, in sight like unto an emerald.'"

"This passage is a turning point in book of Revelation. Before this passage, we see much written about the church. After this passage, the church is not mentioned again until it is presented as the bride of

Christ much later in Revelation. I cannot emphasize this point enough. This event in Revelation Chapter four describes the pre-tribulation rapture of the church."

"Next look at the words used in this passage. 'Come up hither', 'IMMEDIATELY I was in the Spirit', and a 'voice' like a 'trumpet'. Compare these words to the words in First Thessalonians chapter four, verses sixteen and seventeen. 'For the Lord himself shall descend from heaven with a shout, with the voice of the archangel, and with the trump of God: and the dead in Christ shall rise first: Then we which are alive and remain shall be caught up together with them in the clouds, to meet the Lord in the air: and so shall we ever be with the Lord.'"

He then gave several reasons why the next great event would be the rapture. He pointed out First Thessalonians five verses one through nine, stating we are not appointed to wrath. "God will not punish the innocent with the guilty. My God is a just God and cannot do a single thing that is unjust. Therefore, God's children will not have to go through this seven-year period."

He spoke for about an hour, but it seemed like just a few minutes. He then gave an invitation to all who are not sure they would make it to heaven if Jesus would come that night. "If you are not sure you would make it to heaven if Jesus came tonight, you can be sure tonight, you can come to this altar and pray. I like to give people a chance to pray and settle any issues they have. You have a chance to trust Him for your salvation right here and right now."

The altar was flooded with people young and old alike. The church members prayed with them and talked to each about the plan of salvation. I respectfully sat and prayed with them from my pew for about five minutes. I made that commitment many years ago before I married Lisa.

Chapter 2 Tuesday Night at Bible Baptist Church

After service, I stopped in at the fellowship hall to sample the goodies, especially Harriet's dessert. She always fixed the best ones. They were never the same old desserts. Harriet was David's wife. She cared for David about the same way my wife cared for her children. She prepared his lunches for work. David loved to show off all the meals she had fixed him. At work, a daily ritual we all had to go through is watching him go through his large lunch bucket. We all just get lunchmeat sandwiches and chips while he brought out this nine-course meal that would be enough for two people. I guess that is the way she showed her love to him. His portly body revealed that he took in all of her love that she could dish out.

That night, she fixed a cake dessert with a topping that is out of this world. "What is in this topping, Harriet. It is so good!", I asked.

Harriet's face lit up as she described the ingredients of this topping, "I whipped together cream cheese and milk until it was smooth and creamy for the first layer. Then I spread out a layer of crushed pineapple and maraschino cherries. Last of all, I spread out a layer of cool whip and topped it with nuts."

Frank Fuller and his wife, Sondra, came up to the table. Sondra said, "Well, Harriet, it looks delicious, whatever it is!"

If there were ever an opposite of Harriet, Sondra would fill that position. While Harriet does a lot of cooking, Sondra could barely boil water without creating a disaster. Frank and Sondra usually ate out most of the time. It is a good thing that his insurance agency did well so they could afford to eat at so many restaurants. Sondra brought a box of monster cookies from the local Scott's grocery store.

Sondra was a very attractive lady. You could tell that she tended to every detail to make herself look attractive. Her nails were long and usually red, purple, or black, depending on what color matched the dress she was wearing. Her long blonde hair was usually up in some kind of fancy style. She wore strong perfume and usually carried a small, stylish purse that matched her dress. She was always in high heels. Harriet, in contrast, lived a more practical life. Her hair was short, her grey hair was taking over her dark brown hair. She wore, what I would call, comfortable dresses that were very modest. The only working out she did was in her garden and in the kitchen. She had a great beauty in her heart though. I have learned that that is where it counts.

My wife, Lisa, didn't like Sondra because she is afraid that Sondra might somehow seduce me. Of course, Lisa was afraid of any woman that she thought might be more attractive than she was, and some that were not as attractive. After six years of marriage, you would think that Lisa would learn to trust me. That was wishful thinking, I guess.

However, even with all the attention to detail to her appearance, Sondra was still missed some of the things that make a person truly attractive. She rarely smiled with a genuine smile. I am not sure if it was because she was afraid of wrinkles forming or she is truly unhappy. Her attempt to change everything about her natural looks cried out to me saying, "I'm fake."

As Frank and Sondra sat down, Frank asked David, "David, will we be meeting again early tomorrow for our quartet practice?"

David said, "Yes. I think we have the song down well, but we better do it one more time."

Sondra frowned as she heard this news. I think she was more possessive of Frank's time than Lisa was of mine. She didn't like David either, mainly due to the time Frank spent with the quartet. She elbowed Frank, but Frank acted as if he didn't feel it. Frank said, "We'll be here." Sondra rolled her eyes and shuffled in her seat.

I said jokingly, "Well, I know what David will have in his lunch pail for the next couple of days. Hey David, what will go good with that dessert?"

"Anything!" David said with big eyes and a smile. "Hey, Rob. How did you like Dr. Card's message tonight? Pretty good wasn't it?"

"He certainly gave me something to think about. I am still digesting it. It has really made me think about what will happen when Jesus returns." I replied.

"I can remember when I first heard Dr. Card speak about four years ago at a seminar at the First Baptist Church in Lima. I have bought every book and tape he has made since then. I get his newsletter and visit his web site weekly. It is so great to see and hear him live, though. Nothing like it!" said David.

"Well, I am glad you invited me here tonight. I wish I could have brought Lisa. She would have liked it." Well... maybe I lied. I was not so sure that she would like it.

David said, "Well, you will need to drag her out here some night so she can be blessed too." He then began to talk about some of Dr. Card's books and how he could tell that Dr. Card was condensing much of his teachings just to make it fit into the time tonight. That was hard to believe since he was so informative in the hour he had shared with us.

Harriet bent over and whispered to me, "Would Lisa like to have some of this dessert? I'll wrap some up for her."

"She would love some, I'm sure. If not, I'll have something to take to work tomorrow to show the guys. Of course, it might not make it home, Harriet. It is so good."

As Harriet stepped away to get Lisa's cake, David continued to detail issues that Dr. Card didn't bring up in his message that night. "He didn't bring up about what Jesus said in Matthew 24 about the one left and the other left behind. He left out about the comparison Jesus made to the days of Noah. The world was eating, drinking, and marrying until the floods came, just like it will happen when Jesus comes. This world will be going about its business and all the sudden, swish, we'll be outta here!"

He then talked about the Four Horseman of the Apocalypse and detailed what Doctor Card said each of them meant. "Of course, Doctor Card could be covering this in some upcoming services, so I had better shut up about it," David said.

Frank listened intently to David, while Sondra ignored him. She sat there, eating her small plate of food, looking as if she didn't want to be there at all! I saw her roll her eyes occasionally. Harriet, being the best hostess, went to every table in the fellowship hall, making sure that everyone had a piece of her dessert.

As Harriet returned, she handed to me a wrapped foam plate of the dessert, she said, "I put enough on this plate for both Lisa and for your lunch tomorrow, but make sure she gets her share. I will be asking her how she likes it." She looked intently at me like she would find out if I ate it all. I thanked her for the dessert, assured her that Lisa would get a piece of it, and announced to everyone that I had to get home.

Sondra said, "Tell Lisa I said, 'Hi'"

"OK, Sondra, I will." I lied again. I had no intention of telling Lisa. Lisa would just start fuming over how much she can't stand Sondra and how Sondra acted so snobbish and how she wished she had the time and money to do all the things that Sondra does to make herself look pretty. No, I would not let Lisa know Sondra even spoke to me. Life would be much better that way.

David looked up from his plate and asked, with still some dessert in his mouth and on his lips, "Coming back tomorrow?"

I had to turn him down, "Now you know I have mid-week service tomorrow night. I gotta take care of those young people. The church still hasn't found a backup for me yet in case I am sick."

David shouted as I walked out the door, "Hey! Bring them to the Crusade instead!"

I must agree with Lisa, David can be pushy at times, but he is good hearted. In fact, he is one of the best friends a person can have. He doesn't have much money, but he does a lot of good things for those around him. He helped me split some logs last fall for firewood. He likes to find families in need and give them whatever he thinks they need, whether it be clothes from the Salvation Army, toiletry items like toothpaste, toothbrushes, deodorant, or even some of his wife's desserts.

"I'll think about it," I said, with dessert in hand. I really couldn't just say "No," to him. It would delay my trip home even more.

Chapter 3 Tuesday Night at Home

On the way home, I thought about the message. Several thoughts were going through my mind. First of all, I wondered why hadn't I taken the time to study this matter. I reasoned that part of the cause was that I had been busy being a husband, father, and youth leader. As a youth leader, the studies I had taught never dealt much with Jesus' second coming other than as a side issue. Yet, when the altar was opened that night at the revival, I noticed that it was the youth that responded first. I saw them really praying hard and asking for forgiveness. Was I doing my youth an injustice by not dealing with this issue?

I realized that I needed to begin studying scripture to learn what God's Word says about His return. If Dr. Card was right, I needed to prepare my young people for it. What if they were not ready and He comes? Would He hold me responsible? How sad it was to think of those youth missing heaven because of my negligence! As I drove home, I promised God that I would study more about this matter and share this truth with my youth.

As I pulled into the drive, I noticed that all the lights were off except one small light in the family room. I knew that I had missed our children's bedtime and that my wife was reading a book, waiting for me to come home.

Lisa was a good balance to my outgoing, never-know-a-stranger self. She cared a lot about our children. She was a great mother and tended to every need they had, and some they didn't have. She would pour their cereal and milk for breakfast, prepare their clothes for school, fix their snacks for when they came home from school, sewed their clothes, and prepared every meal to their liking. Yet she expected them to do their part as a family member. She had a schedule of chores on the refrigerator door. She kept them on schedule with little exception. There is no doubt in my mind that she loved them. She had what I would call a natural beauty. She didn't need a lot of makeup to look attractive. That was part of what attracted me to her.

David didn't understand Lisa. He said that she worshiped her family and placed them above God. He couldn't figure out why she was not as excited about Dr. Card as he was. "I love her as a sister," he told me once, "but I never did understand my only blood sister either."

Don't get me wrong, he liked Lisa and they were friendly toward each other. They just grated on each other. She thought he was too "pushy", especially when it came to his church activities. "I'm just as good a Christian as he is. I just am not as noisy about it," she often said. I believed her about that. She made sure that the girls said their prayers every night and read their Bibles daily. She read the Bible regularly. She was more faithful to do family devotions than I was. She was faithful to our church and made sure that we tithed... and more. She had been the one that made sure we make it to church each time the doors were open. There had been times that I did not want to go to church, but Lisa kept us going.

I went into the house through the front door and found her curled up in her comforter, reading one of those women's frontier novels for the fourth time. She fantasized about being on the frontier and living a simpler life. I remind her from time to time of the extra work that she would have to do if she lived on the frontier. I reminded her of the cloth diapers (If they had any diapers at all, the washing board, and other lack of conveniences, like a toilet. She then would admit that she wouldn't like it that much. Of course, that next day, she was back into her fantasy.

"Well, it's about time your home," she said, "What took you so long?" I guess that is her way of saying she missed me. She said that same thing if I made a trip to the grocery store and returned home within five minutes.

I handed her the plate of dessert. "Well, you know about Harriet's desserts..."

"Yeah, and David's mouth", she said with a smirk on her face. While I went for a fork, she unwrapped the dessert and looked at it. "What is in this topping? It looks good."

As I handed her a fork, I said, "You'll have to get the recipe from Harriet. I can't remember everything. I think she said something about cream cheese, pineapples, and cherries. By the way, you can't have it all. She sent enough for you to eat and for me to take to work." I continued about the night at David's church while she ate the dessert, "Well, about the Crusade, you know David, he was all excited about the it. He wanted to preach his next sermon right there in the fellowship hall. He even knew about some of the details in Dr. Card's book that he left out of the sermon. He filled us in on every one of them too."

"I bet he did," she said as she shook her head. She took another bite of the dessert and said, "Hey this dessert is great! Too bad you won't have any for lunch tomorrow."

"David will be asking me if I brought it, so you have to leave me half." I said, trying to convince her to leave me some.

"You already had some tonight. In fact, you probably had a couple of servings, haven't you?" I was caught, because I did in fact have two helpings of it. She knows me so well. Lisa asked, "Well, how was this Dr. Card anyway?" She started eating the second serving.

"He really knows his Bible. He believes that Christ could come at any time and that His return will be the next big event. He even had a chart showing every detail of the events that are supposed to happen."

"Well, I hope he is right. The things I see in Revelation are scary to me. I just can't bring myself to read it. I guess it doesn't matter then, since we are Christians and will be gone when all those bad things happen, right?"

"Well, that is what he says."

"Then why waste all that time explaining what isn't going to happen to us? Is he afraid he won't sell enough books?"

I looked at her seriously, "Now, Dr. Card is as sincere a person as I have seen. He also cares a lot about those who aren't ready. You should have seen the young people praying for salvation. They really got help..."

"...or they really got scared" she interrupted.

"Well, God is the final judge of that... How were the kids tonight?"

Lisa went into detail about each one's homework and how Billy was having problems with math. Liz was having problems with being picked on in recess. "You know, they asked where you were tonight. They don't like it when you are not here to tuck them in."

"I know. I just can't be home every night. By the way, we will have to go as a family to this crusade sometime. They have a junior church for our kids. David is expecting you to show up at least once."

Lisa frowned, "I'm not surprised...(She thought for a minute.) OK...One time... Maybe Friday. OK?"

"Sounds good, Honey. Let's go to bed for a few hours before you have to go to work. I wish you didn't have to go to work tonight."

Lisa said, "I do too. But God knows we can't live off of your salary alone."

"I just wish you could be here with me at night instead of being at work."

Lisa patted me on the head, "Well, when you get rich, then we'll talk about that. Until then, I am more than happy to take care of our family by working third shift. I don't mind -—really."

Chapter 4 At Work Wednesday

My mind was on the words of Dr. Card. My body was hung over from all the sugar I had consumed the night before. And my emotions were on edge. I was still concerned about my youth and wanted to spend some time digging into scripture.

David saw my concern at lunch. "What's wrong, did Lisa make you sleep out in the dog house for being out so late last night?" He gave out a loud belly laugh. "I see you don't have your dessert. Did Lisa eat it all?"

I smiled, "You can tell your wonderful wife that Lisa DID eat it all. The good side is that it did keep me out of the dog house. Maybe Harriet will have pity on me and give me another helping." We both laughed. "Actually, the Lord's been dealing with me about something. It's about my youth and their lack of knowledge about end times."

"Boy, did you see the youth that got saved last night? That was great! I love to see young people come to Christ! You say you never taught them about Jesus' coming?"

I replied, "I did, but not in great detail. I've had many other things that I have been teaching..."

"But if you do not teach them about the events of Jesus' return, you are not teaching the whole council of God. You had better get started quick, before He comes. You still have my book I gave you, don't you?"

"Yes"

"Just read it and use it as a study. It will explain everything. The book will save you a lot of time in research too."

"I'll think about it."

"You know, I just can't wait for his return," David said as his voice got louder. "He'll be splitting that Eastern sky one day and then it will be all over!" He started to get excited again, stood and proclaimed to the rest of the lunch room. "We'll be with Jesus then forever!"

Not everyone in the break room shared his enthusiasm. From across the room, I could hear someone say, "Well there must be a revival or something down at the Baptist Church. David is on his lunchbox pulpit again."

"You bet. Doctor Eugene P. Card is here from Virginia Beach, Virginia. He is teaching about Jesus' second coming."

Jim Borkowski looked and asked, "Do you mean Jean Luke Packard from Star Trek? WELL, BEAM ME UP JESUS!" Everyone laughed but David. I even laughed because I never thought about Dr. Card's full name sounding like a Star Trek captain. It was rather funny.

David said, "You won't be laughing when Rob and I are gone and you will be left here to deal with the Anti-Christ. Then you will be sorry for your choice of lifestyle. Turn from your sin and trust in God."

"Every time there is a revival at your church, you do this, David," Ted Longly said scoldingly. "You get all worked up about your Jesus crap and shoot your mouth off."

Jim said, "David, I really do not want to hear about this Jesus coming back thing. I went through that in 1988 and I won't do it again."

I asked, "What happened in 1988?"

Jim replied, "Someone from a church gave me this booklet that told me Jesus would be coming in 1988. The writer had all the facts and figures to prove it would happen way back then. I got caught up into it and started believing it. I got all shook up and was worried about missing the ride to heaven. I ended up quitting my job, because I figured I didn't need it any more. Well, I am still here, with this low paying job to show for it. I am not going to get wrapped up into that junk again. If Jesus wants me, He can find me down at Kelly's Bar on Friday and Saturday nights. That is where I'll be." There were a few snickers.

"I only know one verse of scripture," Ted said. "It says 'Eat and drink for tomorrow we die.' As soon as I fulfill that commandment enough, I'll worry about the others." A few more giggles could be heard from around the lunch room.

"You have been warned. I do not need to say anything else," David said as he sat back down and started eating his lunch. He looked up at me and asked, "Did you laugh at Jim's remark about Dr. Card's name?"

I replied, "You have to admit, Jim has a sense of humor. I wasn't laughing at you. I was laughing at the thought of Dr. Eugene P. Card sounding like Jean Luke Pickard. I'm sorry, David. I just couldn't help it."

"Who is this Pickard guy, anyway? I've never watched any Star Trek shows. I heard that they talk a lot about evolution and alien seed malarky on that show, don't they? You know how I feel about that subject. I had even believed it one time."

"Yes, David, I know. Let's not get started on that one now." I looked at the clock and saw it was 12:30 pm. "Well, it's time to get back to work."

I was relieved that lunch was over. I thought that there might be a fight. I've known Jim for quite some time. He has had a rough life. He lost his father to cancer when he was in high school. He has been mad at God ever since. He has spent a lot of time in Kelly's Bar, drinking his life away and getting into fights. I was surprised to hear that he even tried Christianity at all. It really is sad that every experience he had with God has been bad. But it will only get worse for him unless he turns away from his drinking and accepts Christ in his life. What a sad day it will be when he faces God unless he does.

The rest of that day, I spent thinking about how I should begin studying this issue of Jesus' second coming. I decided as easy as it would be to use Doctor Card's book to study, it would be better for me to do my own study. There is no better place to start than in God's Word. I decided I would check out some online resources to point me to the main verses I needed to study. I knew also that I needed to learn what I could from the book of Revelation also. As I drove the forklift, I prayed for His will to be accomplished. I purposed in my heart to commit myself to study directly from the Bible about this until I was familiar with what God's Word says about His return.

As I did this, I felt God's Holy Spirit touch my heart. I felt a peace like nobody else can give and knew I had His smile of approval. This calm assurance not only let me know His will, but also helped me when I faced David with the fact that I would not be just using Doctor Card's book to teach the youth.

I had always felt it was better to learn biblical truth directly from scripture rather than just to follow someone else's teachings, that it is better to learn biblical truth first hand rather than to just rely on what others say about the scripture. I did this when I studied various subjects. I learned to sit down with my topical bible, an exhaustive concordance, and various translations of scripture and hammer out what the Bible says about a particular subject. I would do this once again after mid-week service tonight when I study about the second coming of Jesus.

Chapter 5 Thursday After Work

At about 5:30 pm, "you-know-who" called. Lisa answered the phone. When she heard who it was, she knew what David wanted. "Just a minute," she said and handed me the phone, along with that look that said that if I go, she would be mad.

"Hi David. Glad to hear from you."

"Are you coming tonight?"

"Not tonight, but we plan on going Friday night. Did you say there was something for the kids to do while we are in the crusade?"

"Yes. We have got the best junior church leaders working with the little ones every night. I am glad you are coming Friday, but you'll miss the Four Horseman tonight. You can see it on my video tapes sometime though."

"Jim was sure sore about the second coming of Jesus today," I chuckled. Jim laughed too. I turned serious and said, "I didn't realize that he had gotten hurt so badly by a false prophecy."

David said, "Yes. It sounds as if he got burned badly by a false prophet. Now I understand a little more why he is so much against anything to do with Church. I will pray that he overcomes those things. Well, Rob, enjoy those little ones while they are young. The day will come when they will be gone and you won't see them anymore. That is if the Lord tarries. God bless you."

"God bless you too," I said as I hung up the phone

Lisa said, "Boy is David pushy. Evidently, someone at work else feels that way too?"

"Yes, Jim Borkowski had a run in with him at lunch. David got a little loud as he does sometimes and Jim got on his case. David isn't all that bad though." I said as I told her what he said about enjoying our children while they are young.

"I am not surprised he said that. He probably drove his children away. He is so pushy! I know I wouldn't want to be in the same house as he. How does Harriet put up with it!? By the way, what do we know about this Dr. Card? Is he really someone we should be listening to?"

I answered, "Well, I still have one of his books that David gave me a few months ago." I pulled his book from the shelf and read the back cover. "His bio says that he graduated from Texas Baptist University. He pastored for 23 years before becoming an evangelist and teacher. He has a long list of references from some rather big names."

Lisa said, "Well, I said I'd go once. That will probably be it. So, what do you want to do tonight? I thought I would get some housework done before work."

"I want to do some deep bible study tonight after we take care of the kids. I promised God I would spend some time reading His Word."

"That's a good thing. I noticed you haven't been spending as much time reading scripture other than preparing your youth lessons and preparing for Sunday School."

"What are you studying?"

"The second coming." I said sheepishly.

"Haven't you had enough of that with David?"

"Well, I want to see it directly from God's Word. You know, without other people's thoughts interjected."

"Well, don't bring that stuff up around me. I don't like it. It scares me."

"Yes dear." I said in my whiniest, wimpiest voice I could muster. She laughed, kissed me and went about her work while I took care of the kids. Billy was still having trouble with math. Liz was buzzing around the room like a bee. Bobby was coloring in some coloring books.

All the time I was playing and working with my children, I was meditating on some verses I read from Matthew 24 last night. It seemed as if much of what I had heard from Doctor Card was there. There was one verse that troubled me, though. "Immediately after the tribulation of those days." Kept ringing over and over in my mind. It seemed as if Jesus was coming after the tribulation if you read Matthew 24:29 for what it says.

Another thing I noticed is that there are some big events that precede His return. It would be hard to mistake what Jesus described happening to the sun, moon, and stars. I also remembered something like an earthquake happening and a sign of the Son of man.

One other thing that really clicked in my mind was the mention of a trumpet at the point of the gathering of the elect. I remembered Doctor Card mentioning about a trumpet in his message from Tuesday night.

Yet that was not what Doctor Card was teaching. He mentioned a sudden disappearance of God's people all over the earth with no warning. He also stated of the rapture being the next great event. He declared that no other events needed to take place before the rapture. This bothered me. I figured that I would spend some more time looking at some other verses to see if more light could be shed on the issue. I prayed that I would gain understanding from His Word. I certainly did not set out to go against Doctor Card, but questions sure were placed in my mind.

After devotions and putting the kids to bed, I sat down to look at the list of verses I wrote down the night before. While reading Matthew, I saw in one of my bible's references to Revelation chapter six. I thought I would check out these references first.

It wasn't long before I realized that I was in the section that dealt with the Four Horseman. The reference I had connected the first seal and the white horse to Matthew 24:6. The next three seals and horses were connected to Matthew 24:7. Matthew 24:9-12 had a reference to

Revelation 6:9-11, which was the fifth seal. The sun, moon, and stars verse, Matthew 24:29 had a reference to Revelations 6:12 and 13. So I sat down and wrote down some of the similarities between these verses. I was amazed how well these two verses paralleled. I saw that the white horse was similar to Jesus' words "war and rumors of war." I saw the red horse taking away peace from the earth being the same as "nation rising against nation" in Matthew. I saw the black horse and the "measure of wheat for a penny" was like the "famines" mentioned in Matthew. I could see the pale horse having some similarities to the "pestilences and earthquakes" mentioned in Matthew.

I saw the tribulation and persecution of the believers in Matthew the same event as the "souls that were slain" in the fifth seal in Revelation, only from a heavenly view. Jesus spoke of the tribulation while in heaven, we see the results of the tribulation, souls in heaven.

What really convinced me that these were speaking of the same event were the sun, moon, and stars parallel I found in Revelation 6:12 and 13. My eyes lit up when I saw this. I wanted to go on, but it was time for bed.

Chapter 6 Friday Night at the Crusade

The Bible Baptist Church was abuzz Friday evening. The greeters were especially friendly tonight. There were conversations going on all over. I noticed that the table that had all of his books and other items was almost empty. A sign said, "If We Are Sold Out of an Item, Please Place an Order."

I saw David and the quartet getting ready for their song as we dropped off the children to the junior church room in the basement. David gave me a big smile as the music began to play for the song the quartet was about to sing.

The sanctuary was nearly full. You could hear the sound of hundreds of people talking. It was so loud that I could barely hear Lisa saying nervously, "There sure are a lot of people here tonight."

"Yes." I said. "There's a lot more here than there was on Tuesday." We found a pair of seats.

The quartet took the stage and sang the song "One Day Too Late".

When they finished, the pastor took the mike and said, "It will be sad for those who miss the rapture. It will be too late for them. They will have to go through the tribulation and face the Anti-Christ. If they are to be saved, they will have to give their lives." He paused and said, "We are glad that all of you are here. There will be a time of fellowship following the services. But you didn't come to hear me. You have come to hear the words of our speaker and hopefully to the Holy Spirit as He speaks to you also. Here is Doctor Eugene P. Card."

The applause was deafening as Doctor Card took the stage. "Thank you, pastor, and thank you for this warm reception. I appreciate the song our quartet sang for us. I would love to bring them along with me as a part of my crusade, but you folks would miss them."

"In our previous night's message, we covered the rapture, the first four seals that were broken, and the Four Horsemen of the Apocalypse, all of this we find in Revelation. We will be continuing with the fifth seal and the sixth seal tonight. First, let's pray for tonight's service."

As the doctor prayed, the people were so quiet you could hear a pin drop. He prayed that God would help him deliver his message and that we would be receptive. When he closed, the crowd in unison said, "Amen."

"The pastor was right when he spoke earlier. It will be a sad day for those miss the rapture and have to go the many terrible things that are mentioned in Revelation. We already talked about the breakdown of all peace, which is a sign that the Holy Spirit has been taken out of the way. I spoke about the terrible famines, pestilences, and earthquakes that will happen in those days. Those days would be terrible enough to endure. But tonight, we will see the worst of the terrible consequences of rejecting Jesus and the salvation He offers. We will look at the martyrdom of those saved after the rapture."

"For those of you who have accepted Jesus Christ as your personal Lord and Savior, you will be spared this terrible tribulation because we know that God will not allow the 'just to suffer with the wicked.' I have hammered this subject quite a bit the first three days of the crusade, so I won't go much further into this issue tonight. Also, I have a lot of verses to deal with and describe tonight."

"The Fifth Seal. You can see this fifth seal on the chart behind me." He pointed to the chart. "As we go down the chart, you can also see Matthew 24:9-12, Revelation 13:15 and 16 as well as a wealth of other verses. Tonight, we will look at the major verses that describe this event.

"Matthew 24 says this: 'Then shall they deliver you up to be afflicted, and shall kill you: and ye shall be hated of all nations for my name's sake. And then shall many be offended, and shall betray one another, and shall hate one another.'"

"Revelation 13 says this: 'And he (speaking of the antichrist) had power to give life unto the image of the beast, that the image of the beast should both speak, and cause that as many as would not worship the image of the beast should be killed. And he causeth all, both small and great, rich and poor, free and bond, to receive a mark in their right hand, or in their foreheads: And that no man may buy or sell, save he that had the mark, or the name of the beast, or the name of the beast, or the number of his name.'"

"The results are Revelation 6: 'And when he had opened the fifth seal, I saw under the altar the souls of them that were slain for the word of God, and for the testimony which they held.'"

"The Antichrist will come and will have enough power in this world to cause all to follow him, no matter what their beliefs. He will temporarily bring peace to the world and cause all to worship him, except for those who believe in Jesus after the rapture. For their 'faith-too-late', as I call it, they will have to pay for it with their lives."

He spent much time describing the Illuminati, the trilateral commission, the skull and crossbones, the masons, and the Bilderberger meetings. He described the power which they have in the world and their ability to effect world events. He linked them to the oil crisis in the 70's, the attempted assassination of Ronald Reagan, and even 9-11. He also told of how they would use a middle east crisis to gain control over the world.

Doctor Card told how the antichrist will rise to power through these organizations and would be "set up" to be the peacemaker in a world hungry for peace. "Once he signs a treaty between Israel and the Arab Nations, a period of peace will follow that will cause others to wonder at his power. At that point, he will claim to be god and establish a new age based religion. The other faiths will follow him because of the peace that was begun. Even some Christian churches will follow him. Those nations that do not follow him will be crushed. Those individuals that will not accept the mark of the beast will be killed."

"I will tell you more about the antichrist tomorrow night. This much I will tell you tonight. The antichrist will come from Rome. He will unite Europe as one nation and will lead the world with the pope at his side as his religious leader. How do I back this up with scripture? Come tomorrow night and see."

"My friends, the most important thing for me to do tonight is to tell you the gospel message. Jesus hasn't come yet and we are still in the age of grace. Jesus died for your sins so that you would not have to go through these terrible events. He died so that you might have eternal life. If you refuse this great gift of eternal life and miss the rapture, you will pay for it with your lives either way. If you refuse the mark, you could die at the hands of the Antichrist. If you accept the mark of the beast, your soul will be damned to an everlasting death in hell. Which do you choose today?"

The altar call was given and the seekers came quickly to the altar for prayer. We left the sanctuary, gathered the children and started home.

The children were tired and fell asleep by the time we got about a block from the church. Lisa was very silent. I asked, "Well, how did you like it?"

"I wish I hadn't come. That Doctor Card scares me. I am scared about what he was talking about. Will our children have to go through that? I know I am saved, but what about my sister and brother? I am glad I have to work tonight. I would have nightmares if I had to sleep."

Chapter 7 Saturday Morning at the Nazarene Church

It was difficult to get up that next morning to go to the men's prayer breakfast, but I really wanted to go so I could have a chance to talk to the pastor about what had been rolling around in my mind concerning the second coming of Christ. Is Doctor Card right or am I just not grasping the truth of scripture? Which stand is biblical?

After I dragged myself out of bed, I shaved, showered and dressed. I drove to the Nazarene Church. The leader of the men's group greeted me warmly at the door. I was glad to see that there were not as many men at the church as I have seen previously. I would have a better chance to pull the pastor aside so I could ask him all those questions that have been rolling around in my mind. When I saw him I made a beeline toward him and said, "Pastor, I have a question for you. Can we talk in your office?"

"Sure. Come this way." Pastor Paul replied.

When we entered in, Pastor Paul closed the door and we sat down. "What can I do for you?"

I explained my problem, "Do you know David, my friend from the Baptist Church?" The pastor shook his head, letting me know he remembered him. "Well, he invited me to see Doctor Card about the Second Coming. Doctor Card certainly gave me a lot of think about. But now I am more confused than I ever was before. Doctor Card teaches a pre-tribulation rapture, but I am finding some different answers from scripture. He is so convincing, but I am not sure I can follow his teaching all the way."

Pastor Paul replied, "People wiser than you and I have held various opinions over this issue for centuries. I have seen all kinds of teachings that say that they are right. I have personally studied pre-trib, mid-trib, post-trib, post-millennial, and amillennial. I too have seen good points brought up about each and I, for a while, didn't know what to think. I couldn't settle on one as a total absolute, but I found a philosophy that has worked for me. Let me see if it will help you. When Jesus came the first time, were the people there ready to accept Him?"

"No." I replied.

"How many were wrong about His first coming?"

"Well, I remember how you taught last Palm Sunday about the fact that many were looking for an earthly king that would save them from Rome. You taught about the word 'Hosanna' meaning 'save us now'. The wise men knew of the birth of Christ, while the rest of Israel were totally unaware. Once they were consulted, the Jewish leaders knew His birthplace was to be in Bethlehem, but they had no idea of what His mission was. The religious leaders didn't know He was the Christ. In fact, they thought he was just a troublemaker and a false teacher. Many of them accused Him of working miracles by the power of the devil."

Then Pastor Paul asked this question, "If the people in Jesus' time were so clueless as to the first coming of Jesus, why wouldn't most of us be just as clueless about His second coming?"

"I see," I said slowly.

"Now don't take this too far. We have been given many details surrounding His second coming and we cannot discount those verses. I believe that they will be fulfilled literally. I will not agree with some thoughts about Jesus' coming when these thoughts are against the literal fulfillment of scripture. Therefore, when I run across a biblical teaching of His return, I look at it as a possibility. In that way, when scripture is fulfilled and an end time event takes place, I will understand it as such because I have not closed my mind to things happening in His time and in His way."

I had to ask, "But which way do you lean? Which one do you think is most biblical?"

"Personally, I lean toward mid-tribulation myself. But I keep my eyes open, because I could be wrong too. Rather than debate on the issue of the timing of Jesus' return, which we are not to know anyway, I focus on what He instructed us to do, to be ready, watch, and pray."

Suddenly a loud knock at the office door broke up the conversation. "Just a minute," Pastor Paul said. He asked me, "Do you understand what I am saying?"

"Yes, I understand"

"Come in," Pastor said to the person at the door.

Tom came in, looking pale, and said, "Pastor, have you looked at your mail yet?"

"No, we don't get the mail until about 10:30. Why do you ask?"

Tom said, "There has been major Anthrax mailing that has many post offices in the country! Come and check out the TV." Both of our phones sounded an emergency alert. They told us not to touch USPS mail and provided a link for the latest news.

We stepped out of the office and into the Family Room, which is our casual room where groups can relax in living room type furniture and watch teaching videos or have bible study. People were looking intently at the TV. I could hear the announcer say, "Apparently, what was thought to be one letter tainted by Anthrax turned out to be a bulk mailing was sent out from Indianapolis, Indiana that was laced with the Anthrax virus. This mailing apparently was sent to Mayors in major cities throughout the country. This mailing could potentially infect every post office since these letters went to each of the central post offices in the country."

"One letter is being examined by the FBI as we speak to determine who sent it and whether it is indeed Anthrax. I am getting word that the white house spokesman, Thomas Sawback, is getting ready to give us the results of the investigation...here he comes to the mike."

I saw the stern look on Mr. Sawback's face as he approached the mike. "Ladies and Gentlemen of the press, it is my duty to inform you of the details of what we have uncovered in this mailing. First, it has tested positive for Anthrax. It is in a highly refined form of Anthrax and has the appearance of white powder. The worst finding of all is that the envelope has been perforated at the top in order to enhance the spread of the Anthrax virus throughout the mailing system. It appears that the intent of the letter was not only to infect the mayor's office with the anthrax virus, but also to maximize the ability of the letter to spread anthrax onto other letters in the postal system as the sorting machines in the major post offices processed them. Each time these letters were handled, whether by machine or by hand, they spread the virus. Each time they were squeezed or bent, air was forced out the perforations a the top of these envelopes, infecting anyone near this envelop as well as any letter near it or following it."

"It is probable that the perpetrators of this crime intended to infect not only the mayors of each town, but to create country wide panic. The end result is that every post office must be evacuated and every piece of mail must be inspected for anthrax."

"We have details as to when this mailing went out, but we are not sure where each letter went to. As of now, do not handle any mail that was received Friday or today. Dispose of any mail in the last two days into a sealed plastic bag and wash your hands thoroughly."

"The FBI has information about who sent these letters and are pursuing those responsible for this horrible crime."

"The president is safe and is not in harm's way at this time. All mailrooms in Washington DC have been shut down until further notice. We are not ready to give any more information at this time. No questions please at this time."

Pastor Paul stepped in front of the TV to speak to us. "Please mute the television for a minute." The TV became silent. "I am just as shocked as you are. This act of terrorism deeply saddens me." He paused to compost himself. "We need to pray. We do not know what will happen in the future. We don't know who even among us might be infected. We need to pray for our country, for its leaders, for those infected and for ourselves. If you need to call home or feel the need to go home, please do so." Then the pastor prayed.

After his prayer, the television was turned back up. As the news was continuing, I texted Lisa to not get the mail, just in case and told her to turn on the news. The news anchorperson talked about the possible source of anthrax. There was much speculation about who it could be. He then paused, visibly disturbed. "I am hearing reports of a bombing in a Jewish synagogue in New York. We have reporters on the way to the scene. Please stand by as we give you the latest."

I decided I had better go home to see if Lisa was OK and to comfort her and the kids. On the way home, I turned on the radio.

There was no new information. Just a repetition of the same information that was revealed earlier, along with speculation as to who did it and what their motives were. Once I pulled into the drive, I went into the house. Lisa was playing a game with the kids on the living room floor. She said, "There was nothing on TV for them to watch, so I turned it off and we started to play a game." She tried to smile, but the concern on her face let me know she had heard. She wanted to protect our children from the terrible news.

"Do you want me to join in on a game or should I get lunch ready?" I asked. I was trying to act cheerful while at the same time taking care of some important information with Lisa. I had to get rid of yesterday's mail as soon as possible.

Lisa said, "Why don't you wash up, and then join us? The mail is on the counter next to the kitchen table."

I took a garbage bag from the drawer, used it to pick up the mail, and placed it into the garbage bag. I then took a washcloth and wiped down the counter and discarded it also. I took the bag out and put it in the trash container. I thought through the possibilities of where the mail had been and thought to sanitize the front door handle. I was glad that neither of us had time to go through the mail yesterday since we went to see Doctor Card last night, but the thought of that virus being in our house was an eerie feeling. It could have been picked up off the floors and spread throughout our house. If it did, then playing on the floor would be a horrible place to play a game. I said as casually as possible, "I just wiped down the table and counter. Let's go out there and play the rest of the game. It is safe out there. Lisa, did you want to see the TV while the kids and I play?"

"Sure, Rob."

I collected the game and we set up the game on the kitchen table. One good thing about having the kids is that they can help keep you distracted when you are burdened. I enjoyed the next hour, playing games with the children while Lisa listened to the news. She had it loud enough that I could hear the constant repetition of the same news that I had heard earlier while I played with the children. The only change was an update periodically that would show a live report from various locations in the country where the letters were sent to.

Lisa decided she had heard enough news and turned off the television. She asked the children if they wanted to go to the park. They excitedly put away the game and were ready to go within about two minutes. Lisa said, "Would you like to stay here and see if there are any changes in the news while you warm up dinner? We will be at the park until about noon. All you need to do is place the large dish in the oven at 10:30 on 325 degrees. It will take care of itself."

I nodded and my family left to go to the park. I called David. "Have you heard the news today?"

David said, "I sure have. I bet that it was those Muslims that did that. Don't you think, Rob."

"I am not sure, but it sounds like a well thought up plan, whoever did it. I wouldn't jump to the thought of Muslims right away though. That sounds really racial." David explained that he was going to hear what Doctor Card had to say about it tonight. I agree that it would be interesting to hear his perspective.

Just then, another alert went off on my phone. I quickly said goodbye to David.

Chapter 8 American Nightmare

I turned on the television and checked my phone. A national emergency was declared. All were to stay home and take shelter and watch the latest news on the radio or television station designated for emergencies.

As I watched the news, there was a "breaking news" bulletin. A bright flash of light was seen in the direction of New York City that could be seen from Scranton, New York. At the same time, all connections were lost to New York City and the surrounding area as far away as Edison, New Jersey. They had a complete blackout.

Then there was another breaking news. The same thing happened in several major cities all over America. There was a bright shining light followed by a complete blackout. There are no communications coming from of these cities: New York City, Philadelphia, Los Angeles, Houston, and San Diego.

On the TV... "Hi, I`m Carlie Azuz. We are thankful your taking time to watch it. Let`s just jump right in with the details. There are reports all over the United States of bright flashes of lights over some of the top cities in the United States, all at about the same time. Among the cities that experienced this at this point is New York City, Los Angeles, Houston, San Diego, Chicago, and Philadelphia. At the same time, all electricity and phones have shut down. Conversations were cut off. Television broadcasts have stopped. Live YouTube and Facebook broadcasts were cut midstream. The question is, "What just happened? To answer this, I have a nuclear scientist, Dr. William Steinberg, from

Boston University on with me to explain what this phenomenon might be. Thank you, Dr. Steinberg, for helping us to make sense out of all this."

Dr. Steinberg: "Carlie, thanks for having me on here. I am glad to shed some light on this issue."

Carlie: "You are welcome. So, what do you make of these events?"

Dr. Steinberg: "Now, of course, it is just speculation at this point, but it appears to be a nuclear blast that was set off just a short distance off the ground. This would cause an electromagnetic pulse that would interfere with any object that uses computer chips for miles around the blast. We are talking about things like cellular phones, computers, and even vehicles. This is why communications were cut off from these areas. Cellular phones were probably frying in the hands of the users as they were talking. This would also cause power outages in these areas due to power line insulator failures."

Carlie: "A nuclear blast? Over many of our major cities? How does this effect the people there? What medical problems are they facing?"

Dr. Steinberg: "It would all depend on the height of the explosion and the strength of the blast. There is no way of knowing. I am sure they will be in need of medical assistance."

Carlie: "So, are first responders being sent?"

Dr. Steinberg: "It is my understanding that there are a large number of first responders driving into these cities as we speak."

Carlie: "Thank you for coming on to help us make sense of what is happening."

Dr. Steinberg: "Any time."

Carlie turned to the camera: "So now you have heard it. It is presumed that a nuclear blast that went off simultaneously in five major cities throughout the country. Back to you, Jake."

Jake: "Thank you Carlie. We have some footage to share with you that might reveal some more information. There was a live broadcast that was being sent from Los Angeles that might reveal some more information. As you can see, a missile was seen rising from direction of the Pacific Ocean and a bright light coming from this missile, and then the feed was cut off."

I left the television continue as I started warming up dinner. They repeated over and over, as they usually do, repeating the same information, occasionally showing more video that revealed more of the same information I had already seen.

I stopped after putting the dinner in the oven and prayed for the people in the cities involved, for the responders that will be driving into harm's way shortly, and for our country as a whole. I began to weep for our country, unsure of what was going to happen.

The phone rang, David was on the other line. "Did you hear about what has been happening? God is coming soon!"

I responded, "It sure looks like big things are happening. I haven't felt like this since 9-11. I was just praying as you were calling."

David, "I was just on my knees too! Now, I really can't wait to get to see Dr. Card tonight! You coming?"

I responded, "No.... we are supposed to be staying home according to the emergency alerts. I know my wife will want me home tonight to be here for her and the family. How about if I watch the news for anything new while you hear what Dr Card says if you can do it without getting arrested. They may even not hold services due to this emergency. We can get each other caught up when you get home. OK?"

David, "In fact, I will stop in to see you in person. Even better?"

"As long as you keep it quiet, our kids will be in bed by then. It might help Lisa to hear what Dr Card said."

"That's a deal! God bless you, my brother!"

I heard the children coming to the front door, laughing and giggling as they came in the door. I greeted them with open arms and gave them all a group hug, as I have always done in the past. I am so grateful to God for Lisa, who tries her best to keep the kids innocent.

Lisa gave me her nervous but satisfied smile. As the kids went to get cleaned up, I updated her on the events of the day. Lisa said, "It's not getting better, is it? Did you get the alert?"

"Yes, I did get the alert. No, it isn't getting better. I was asked to go with David to Dr. Card's meeting. I agreed with him that I would keep track of the news for all of us. He is stopping after the meeting, if they have it, to share with us what Dr. Card says about what was happening. I hope you don't mind." I looked at her intently, hoping she wouldn't object.

She replied, "As long as he is quiet. The kids will be sleeping by then." She looked at me with concern. I knew what she was going to say.

I began to laugh. "That was my first response to him when he suggested about coming over. I told him to be quiet."

She smiled, "I have you trained so well." We hugged and kissed. "At least I have you!"

The children began to come into the kitchen with us. The dinner was ready, so we had the children set the table for the meal. The roast was brought out and placed in the middle of the table. We sat down, one of the children said prayer, and we began to eat.

Chapter 9 Apocalypse

After dinner, Lisa started playing with the Nintendo Switch 3 with the children so I could continue watching the news. This was a good thing, as I think back on it.

As I watched the news, I could hear the laughter from the family room while I watched the news on my Samsung notebook phone. I put in my earbuds so I could hear the news without accidently exposing the kids to the negative events of the day.

Jake was still on the broadcast, repeatedly playing the same videos that I saw earlier, with a few new ones added. I guess I volunteered for this torture, so I can't complain.

Jake: "So, we can see that Dr. Steinberg was right in his earlier broadcast. Nearby EMS units as well as medical and battle-ready units from the military went into the cities attacked by the bombs earlier, which rumor has it, came from North Korea. I say "rumor" because we cannot get confirmation from government officials. They are being rather hush hush about everything, which makes me nervous." He put his hand up to his ear, as if he was listening to his earpiece and said, "I am being told that the president of the United States as getting ready for a statement soon, so we will go live to the Whitehouse press room for this statement.

The press room was abuzz, with several of the members of the press talking to each other. The Secretary of State stepped up to the mic and announced that the president would be coming soon for his statement.

Jake stepped in to speculate what the president was going to say. It was more like he was just filling in the dead space.

"The President of the United States" was announced a few minutes later.

President Pence came out to deliver his address, "My fellow Americans, we have experienced the most horrifying attacks on the United States since 9-11 today, so as my job as president is to let you know what I know and can share. It is clear that North Korea has chosen to attack the US directly with several high-powered nuclear bombs in an attempt to cripple us economically and morally. The bombs that were used to attack our largest coastal cities were fitted with bombs that were strong enough to knock out all communication to everyone within a fifteen mile area of the explosion. They were launched from Russian subs just off the coast of each city. There was no warning and our defenses were unable to stop these missiles since it only took a few short minutes from the time the missiles were launched and the explosion took place. I am not at liberty to say what our reaction will be, but it will be swift and sure. Vice President Owens is safe and in an undisclosed location for now."

"Our early warning system DID stop a missile from hitting here in Washington D.C.. That is the only reason we are able meet here today. We have spared many lives and I thank God for that."

"Having said that, following this meeting, I will be sheltering in the bunker provided for myself and my immediate staff so that is the worst happens, we will be prepared and we will be able to function. The public deserved to know what was happening first. We don't know what to expect in the future. We do not know what is planned by our enemies, so we are preparing for the worst. We also are under martial law until further orders. Only essential personnel are allowed out of their homes. This lockdown is to prevent further problems and protection in case of a nuclear attack."

"We haven't received word of an attack yet, but until the "smoke clears" from this last event, we are being cautious. Thank you all and God bless America." He immediately left the stage with his staff. The reporters asking unanswered questions at a loud pitch."

Jake started repeating what was said by the president. My thoughts were too loud in my head to hear what he was saying. Then I saw a series of videos of ICBM's lauching. I looked at where they were taking off from. North Dakota, Montana, and Wyoming was where the feed was coming from.

I got another alert. It advised me to take shelter due to a nuclear attack. I gathered the family and we went down to the basement. The children were frightened. Lisa spoke to them calmly to help them to relax. I pulled out my phone and continued to watch the news with my ear buds. This was one time that I was glad Lisa insisted on having a basement.

According to the news, several countries had launched ICBM's. It would be just a few short minutes until it would be all over. I lead in prayer. "Father, You are not surprised by the events happening right now, but we are. First of all, we thank you for Who You are. You are gracious, loving and kind. You are near to us in our times of trouble. We are troubled right now. We ask for forgiveness for any wrongs we might have committed. Forgive us for all of our sins. Cleanse us with the blood of Your Son, Jesus Christ. We ask that You would spare us from this tragedy. Unless You intervein, we will all be blown up. Perform Your miracle, as only You can do. In Jesus' Name we ask it. Amen. The family all responded with an "Amen."

Billy asked me, "Why would God do this to us?"

I responded, "It wasn't God that set off those missiles. It was men that chose to do it. You see God gave each of us free will to do whatever we wish. We all have done wrong things with these choices. Do you remember some wrong choices you have made?" Billy looked down and shook his head up and down. "We have these choices so that we can have the free will to choose Him. God didn't want robots to serve Him. He wanted us to have free will so we could freely worship Him. Don't hold anything bad that happens to us against God. If you want to be angry at anyone, be angry at Satan. He is the one who steals, kills, and destroys. Understand?"

"I understand. I just wish that this wouldn't have to happen."

"Billy, I love you."

"Love you dad."

"Liz", waiting until she looked up at me, "I love you too."

I looked at Lisa, smiling, "You know I love you!"

"Bobby, I love you too."

Bobby just smiled and shook his head.

"At times like this, I especially love you." We did a group hug as they all told each other they loved them.

I then heard shouts of joy and cheering. They said a miracle had happened...

Chapter 10 Apocalypse Diverted

We all huddled around the cell phone as they were telling what happened. All over the world, the missiles just disappeared, preventing a worldwide nuclear holocaust.

Jake explained, "Just before the missiles hit their target, they appeared to fly into a circular shaped disk and didn't come out on the other side. It was like they disappeared into another dimension. Thanks to our brave news crews around the world, we have several of these accounts on video, which we will air as soon as we can."

"The big question is, 'Who is responsible for this kind act?' Was it an act of God? Was it some kind of technology we were unaware of that our military had? We hope to find out soon. Here is our first feed."

My first thought as I saw the missile looming closer to the cameraman was that he truly was a brave man. You could see the missile getting larger at a great rate of speed. Then a circle of darkness appeared in front of it and it disappeared into the circle. The video then panned to the right, revealing the source of the circle... a flying saucer. A UFO! It then disappeared out of sight.

Jake had a look of shock on his face as the footage repeated in a split screen, "Friends, you have just seen the miracle take place. We were saved.... by aliens! At least that is what it looks like. I don't know how else to describe it. Well, here's more footage."

This video was from Moscow. It was from an airplane. It showed what I would assume one of our missiles. A UFO appeared, created the dark circle in front of the missile with something like a beam, the missile disappeared into that dark circles and vanished. Just like in the earlier footage, the flying saucer disappeared at a high rate of speed.

Lisa and I looked at each other with shock. I asked, "Well, I didn't expect deliverance THAT way, did you?"

Lisa just looked at me, eyes bulging and shaking her head no. "That is just so weird! But we both ARE alive because of whoever or whatever that that was."

I could hear gun shots, fireworks and shouting outside. It sounded like it was a good type of shouting, so we ventured out of the basement. The neighborhood was ecstatic. Some were drinking. Others were dancing. I won't talk about what some were doing on their front lawn, but they were all having their own way of celebrating. Whether we had martial law or not, I don't think anyone cared.

We brought the family inside the house. I decided to thank God for another day of life. I couldn't help but wonder about these mysterious UFO's though. What were they? Where did they come from? I smiled at Lisa. I could tell she was nervous yet because she forced a smile back at me. While it appeared that an apocalypse was diverted, I am sure this wasn't the end of it all. She was feeling this weight too. Our phones went off with another alert, stating that the president would be sending out a message soon.

The kids were hungry, so we all went into the kitchen to fix something to eat.

As we were engaging each other, fixing sliced turkey sandwiches, I couldn't help but wonder the meaning of all this. Part of me was happy, like those celebrating outside, that we were delivered from sure destruction. However, I too wondered who or what delivered us.

As the children were enjoying their sandwiches, I went into the living room to see if the president was on yet. He was already talking. I turned up the volume. He was in a totally different place than I have ever seen a president speak from. I would presume that it was from the bunker that he spoke of earlier. "It is clear that humanity was on a path of destruction. We had, all across the world, felt forced to settle for mutual destruction. All other options were considered, but when missiles were launched at us, we were forced to retaliate by sending our ICBM's to North Korea and Russia. I was living the nightmare that every president had since Harry S Truman."

He paused as he fought back his tears, "At the last minute, an unknown force rescued us from destroying ourselves. We owe our thanks to whoever that was. I cannot express enough gratitude for these entities. All of the countries around the world received communication from them to cease fire and as far as I know, every country has complied with these orders. I CAN speak for our country and say that we will comply and stand by."

"We are still keeping our country in a state of martial law until we can be sure of everyone's safety. Our Emergency Planning Agencies have stepped up to the plate and have put into place the plans they have needed to in order to best assure our safety. After this crisis has subsided, we will reconsider our stand on martial law."

"In the communication from those who saved us from destruction, we were also told to stand by for a broadcast from them." He raised his eyebrows and tilted his head, "Hopefully, we can get some answers from them. Until then, we will simply need to wait."

Lisa and the children began to play a video game in the family room, enabling me to continue watching the news. Laughter could be heard from the family room over the low volume of the television, so I turned the television up a little. The president's speech was over. The news began to recite the speech of the president, working and churning the meaning of every word that was said.

Suddenly, the television began to have its signal interfered with. Lines were forming across the screen. The audio portion became scratchy. I could tell as the signal came back to the news, that the news people had stopped their usual yammering and they were informing us about how their teleprompters were malfunctioning, effected by some kind of interference.

Lisa complained from the family room, "Rob are you playing with the television? We can't play our games if you keep messing with it."

"I am not doing anything to your TV, but something is happening to everyone's screens on the news too. It is something beyond us. Just wait. Maybe it will clear up." Just then, an image came on the screen. It looked human-like, but the skin was pale, looked like the skin of a catfish, and was spotted in a pattern with black oval shapes. The skull was narrow and the very high cheek bones. The eyes were dark and larger than a human eye. Even though this creature was strange looking, he had a warm smile on his face...

Chapter 11 Enkilo's Greeting

"Hello, my name is Enkilo. I am a leader of my race, the Ebgalians. My friends and I have been watching your world for a long, long time. We have noticed the direction your society has been taking, especially in the last century. You humans have become increasingly more violent and dangerous as your knowledge has increased. This has been your pattern over the millenniums."

"This pattern is due to your DNA. You are not be able to help yourselves since your DNA has been altered. I blame myself and those who helped me to improve your chromosomes so your ability to learn would increase. We have revealed ourselves at this time because there was no other choice in order to save your race and this world."

"In times past... a long time ago... we had been more directly involved with your species, it was wonderful to see you utilize the advanced technology we offered. Your ancestors built some wonderful structures with our technology. Many that have lasted to this day. All over the world, you have the evidence of these massive buildings that have lasted for all these millenniums. Your scientists and engineers have marveled at how their ancestors were able to construct such large edifices with such heavy materials with the accuracy and detail that they have been constructed.'

"Once we revealed these methods of design and construction to your ancestors, you humans were quite unstoppable. You created building after building, each with a variation that revealed your ability to use your imagination. You had the drive to accomplish, which was always a part of your original design."

Your ancestors began to beg for more knowledge because you realized how limited your original design was. They kept insisting, and we finally relinquished. We modified your DNA so you would have a greater capacity to learn. We were successful, but it came with a cost. A darker side of your personality was formed.

To this date, there is a part of you that wants to do good. There is a part of you that is self-driven despite what might be good for others. Freud called it the "Id". Your Christian faith calls it the "sinful nature". Many of you have described that as the "devil on one shoulder and the angel on the other." When we increased your knowledge, that bend toward selfishness also came with it."

"Your tendencies toward egotism put you on the path of destruction back then just as it did today. Instead of using the new capacities we designed within you to advance your race, you began to be self-destructive. You used our technology to kill one another and many of the other animals in your world. We felt pity on you and wanted to help you to grow as a race. We had been so proud. But things grew worse for you. You became so destructive that some of us even began to complain and show remorse that we had brought this upon you."

"One of the Ebgalians, that had not been on earth, got wind of the modifications we had made. He was angered about what was done and decided to destroy the earth with a flood. Your myths have recorded many versions of all this. My favorite version because of the accuracy is the Sumerian tablets. This one who planned to destroy the earth was called "Enlil" in the tablets. I was called "Enki." Enlil successfully brought a flood on the earth, but I was able to save some of you from this destruction. You were able to rebuild your lives."

"We vowed to not allow you to use the building technology we had given to you before the flood. Enlil also joined us in trying to help you improve yourselves. Once, after the flood, your ancestors began to build a great tower like they had seen done in the past before the flood. Enlil struck down the building so they would give up on building great edifices as they had in the past."

"Enlil attempted to help your race in many ways to fight against your evil tendencies through his instructions which you can find in the Bible. He appealed to your better side to strengthen what Freud called your superego. This has become your monotheistic religion and faith."

"In the more recent past, we had thought your race was improved enough that you could handle more of our technical knowledge, so we allowed you to have one of our ships that accidently crashed so you could see how it operates. I think you call it "reverse engineering." You were able to make great advancements in your technology with your findings... to a point." He developed a frown on his face, "You were misusing this technology. You took our fiber cables and instead of using it to advance yourselves as a race, you strung the fiber cables all over and used it for "entertainment." You also took one of our most useful products which you call mylar and made balloons and snack wrappers out of it. We knew then that you weren't ready for us to share more with you at that point."

"You have seen our ships in several places in your history. There are many sightings you have recorded, although we were trying to be "incognito."

We interceded at your Chernobyl nuclear accident. If we had not intervened, there would have been a destructive blast that would have been devastating for your people. We were able to bring down the radiation levels through the same means as we stopped your day of disaster today. We have the ability to change time and space and were able to remove the dangerous nuclear materials from Chernobyl and place it into another part of the galaxy, where it could do no harm."

"The purpose of this communication is to reveal that we want to help you. We do not have any ill intent for you. We are only coming to you as a last resort, to keep you from destroying yourselves, this wonderful world you live in, and to try to help you overcome your evil intentions. More on this later."

"There are so many other details that I would love to share with you... and I will reveal these details at a later time. We simply wish to let you know that we have your best intentions in mind so that as we reveal more about ourselves, you will not be distressed."

"I ask that you would trust us with your future." He leaned toward the camera and frowned, "Need I remind you that the only reason you are hearing this message is due to our intervention in your self-destruction. As we reveal ourselves, we ask that you would keep all of this in mind." He smiled and reassured, "We are here to help you. Please trust us. We will become more open about our presence on the planet soon. As we do so, we don't want you to be frightened and panic. We too have seen how you have dealt with aliens on your movies and TV shows." He smiled and said, "We want you to see us like Elliot saw ET. I like Elliot. You should all try to be like Elliot."

"One of us will give you more details about where we have been and what we have been doing as we have tried to remain undercover. Be watching for our many appearances around the globe and please do not be alarmed."

The TV phased out from Enikilo's transmission and back to Jake, who just stared at his monitor...

Chapter 12 Reactions

Jake realized that he was back on the air and began to talk, "I am entirely speechless. Never in my life did I ever think I would sit before you all after such an incredible series of events. There was no training for this type of incident." He put his hand to his ear. "I am being told that we have a professor from Houston up next that is willing to share some observations. I'm gratefully for this because I am still dumbfounded... Chet?"

Thank you, Jake. Also thank you for staying with us during this crisis. You look like you can use some rest." Chet turns to the person next to him. "I have Dr. Harmon here from Houston NASA Propulsion to talk to us about the events of the last day. Doctor, what you can share with us about what we have seen?"

"As an expert in rocket propulsion, I actually have more questions than answers. However, I have been able to study the type of missiles were used in the attacks. I can tell you that they were from the United States, Russia, North Korea, and China. In other words, every major country that had nuclear ICBMs had used them in this assault. In reviewing the timing of the missiles, it is probable that North Korea was the first to launch their missiles. After that, it was hard to know the sequence of the launchings, but in the end, it looks like they all had launched their initial rounds of missiles."

"You mean there are more missiles out there to be launched?" Chet asked, with great concern.

"Oh yes. It is estimated that there are enough nuclear missiles left to blow up the world at least five more times. I think that is why the Ebgalians communicated to all the countries to cease launching any more missiles. They also knew that there was still a danger of more nuclear destruction."

"So, Doctor, what did the Ebgalians use to cause all those missiles to disappear?" Chet inquired.

"Now THAT is far beyond my expertise and beyond most expert's expertise. I presume the Ebgalians have abilities that go far beyond the capacity of any of us. We seem to able to effect space and time to transport the missiles into another galaxy, another time, or another "realm", if you will. Since they were able to handle this crisis so easily, I presume they could do the same in any situation. Where did the missiles go? Maybe they can explain that one, if he chooses to."

Chet turns to the camera, "The biggest question still goes unanswered. Maybe Enikilo CAN answer us. Maybe he cannot. Hopefully he is listening and WILL answer our questions."

My phone rang, making me jump. You can guess who was on the other end. David was so exuberant; I could barely grasp was he WAS saying. "David, slow... down... a little. I can't understand."

"I'm sorry, Rob." David said a little more calmly. "I am just so wired up because of this alien's speech. Did you noticed how he backed up scripture about the flood, and the tower of Babel... and the sinful nature? He also took a shot at evolution and the entertainment industry. I am wondering if these creatures aren't angels who came here to bring about the salvation of mankind. I have been listening to some broadcasts about the Visitors. They are saying the they are actually angels. Now the world will say that they are just aliens. That Giorgio guy is being hailed as the one guy who had it right. Also, the Raelians are being hailed as a true prophet."

"Giorgio?"

"The guy on the TV show, Ancient Aliens. He had the crazy hair that stuck up. At least he DID have hair. Since then, he shaved his hair since he went partially bald. I am so glad I watched them shows to keep up on what they were saying."

I recalled, "I remember that guy. I thought he was just crazy. The hair removed every doubt in my mind. Now they are thinking he's 'all that'?"

"Yep. Along with all the others that were on that show. Most of them have passed away since they did the show, but this Giorgio guy is still alive and doing press releases like crazy. He just doesn't look the same without the wild hair."

"So what are the Raelians?"

"They are a group of people that said that the ones that really created us were aliens. They did some human cloning at the turn of the century that gained them some notoriety."

I had to ask, "So what do you think of everything that Enikilo had to say? There are a lot of red flags for me. He may have shared some scriptural references, but there are several issues that he brought up that don't seem very biblical."

David didn't care much for my questions. David sternly said, "I believe that he will explain more later. I don't know much about the Sumerian tablets, but they sound good. I seem to remember Giorgio saying something about them. I am also checking out the Raelians. What they are saying has come into play today!"

For the first time, I realized that David was an easily swayed person. I had always seen him as a big time Christian. It appears now that he seems to be attracted to Christ for a long time. All this talk about Dr Card was simply who he had followed for a long while. He definitely had the shiny penny syndrome. Hopefully, David will come to his senses.

Chapter 13 The "Beast" from the Sea

In some ways the news channel had a typical day. Talking about the past events. Trying to gain new insight from the clues left by Enikilo. Prognosticating the future events. One thing that was different today though. A tip was given to keep an eye on the Persian Gulf, so the news media are also speculating what THAT means. Drones were sent out, scouring that body of water.

One of the drones picked up some underwater motion in the clear waters of the Persian Gulf. Other drones were sent and focused on the event. There was evidence that the waters were being displaced, creating two waves of water that spread out to each shore. This happened all the way up the gulf. Since the water was clear, a craft of some sort was visible under the water.

At the end of the gulf, suddenly the ship appeared out of the water. It had a sleek appearance. The front of the ship was larger and taller than the rear. There were windows all over the main body ship. As the ship hovered above the earth, its landing pads came out. Each pad had four large "hooks". The sound of the ship was a loud, deep hum. There were no rockets used to propel the ship. The ship hovered above the ground as it slowly made its way up to its final destination, southeast of Abadan, Iraq. It landed at a remote area just outside of town. When it landed, the outstretched landing pads lowered the main body to the ground.

Thanks to the drones, we have some great footage of the spaceship, if that's what you call it. From a distance, the windows on the body looked like spots. The bulky top didn't have windows except on the front. There was a wrap-around window on the lower part, with two front-facing windows on the upper section. My guess is that the main control room is where the wrap around window is. It resembled the Egyptian Sphinx. Could it be THAT is why they made that the sphinx in Egypt?

The media vans arrived shortly after the landing and the reporters readied themselves for the encounter. Once the dust settled, a door opened in the front of the ship between the two landing pads and a few creatures stepped out. They seemed to have the same appearance as Enikilo. The reporters quickly adjusted their cameras and mics. The creatures walked out from between the pads and waved to the cameras. One of the creatures came to the microphones and began to speak. "Peace be with you, my dear friends. Do not be afraid. We mean you no harm. Enikilo shared with you two days ago that we would reveal ourselves to you and that you should not be alarmed. I am Enmedigo. I am the leader of the military of the Ebgalians."

"Although I am the leader of the Ebgalian military, we are not here today as a military action. We have returned to what you call "the cradle of civilization". This is where you humans were first located and where we interacted with your ancestors many millenniums ago. This ship is one of our combat ships that we used in the past for defensive purposes. Fortunately, we haven't had to use it in that capacity lately."

Enmedigo turned and pointed toward one of the others that stood behind them. "Anneduga was the one that trained your ancestors on how to build the great edifices that you have discovered around the globe." Anneduga closed his eyes and nodded his head forward in a greeting fashion. "Your forefathers learned quickly and were very productive. We were so pleased with your progress and felt compassion for your race. We have returned here, where it all started in order to give you another chance. We have learned much about your species and how we can help you. Believe me, if we didn't care for you so much, we wouldn't have bothered with saving you from your Armageddon a few days ago."

In the midst of the crowd of onlookers, a shout was heard. "You are the Beast from Revelation!" A man with a gun moved forward from the crowd, aiming his rifle and firing on Enmedigo. Enmedigo dropped to the ground. A glow came from the front part of the ship and a beam went down to the shooter. The beam disappeared and the shooter, as well as the ground around him, disappeared. All that was left was a bowl-shaped hole in the sand.

Meanwhile, the Ebgalians picked up their wounded comrade and they hurried back into the ship, leaving the reporters and bystanders looking at each other. The reporters closed out their broadcasts. Most of the drones left their stations and only a few remained, watching the ship. A few reporters also stayed behind to keep us abreast on anything new that might happen.

The scariest fact is that everything on the Ebgalian ship was shut down. Every window but the ones on the front top were closed. It looked like a lion, looking toward Abadan. The Iraqi military roped of the ship so nobody would come close to the ship.

Chapter 14 The Media Blitz

For three days we receive a blitz of news reports. They identified the man with the gun as a "Christian sympathizer". His Facebook was examined to reveal that he called himself a Christian. Psychiatrists were quick to analyze him as a radical right-wing Christian that held conservative beliefs about the Bible.

Then came the editorialists. Rather than seeing this man as a "Lone Wolf" like they do for most of the terrorists, they chose to condemn all of Christendom because of the actions of one man. This was all they needed to condemn all of Christianity.

Makenzi Pilit is one of the worst. In her world, the worst thing you can be is a male Christian. Of course, society has backed this mentality for a long time. She took every opportunity to make this event a new reason to stereotype and condemn the Christian cause. "What we really need to do is regulate these fanatics. They are the ones that are holding us back as a society! Now, I am not saying that all Christians should be scrutinized. There are many of the older Christian faiths that have come to the realization that the Bible is a dangerous book that cannot be taken literally. But these literalists are so dangerous. If the Ebgalians decide to end the world tomorrow because of this bible crazed man, I couldn't blame them. But why should we all suffer because of one person?"

All I can say is, WOW! She is willing to condemn all of real Christian faiths for the actions of one, but then complains that it isn't fair that all of humanity would suffer for the actions of one man. That is ironic, and tremendously inconsistent. Others joined in with her condemnation.

Those that hold to the anti-God agenda have targeted, infiltrated and took over Texas. Now, Texas is voting along with California and New York. It won't take much for a nation to cram their agenda down the rest of our country, whether we want it or not because of those three states. One more crisis will give them the excuse they need.

Due to the actions of this one that was not even an American, the defamation of all biblical American Christians just got worse. The worst of the persecutors are those who claim to be Christians, but have rejected clear biblical teachings and have clung to new age teachings.

The shooter's name was Abal Kristos an Iraqi missionary from The Ethiopian Biblical Methodist Church. This is not to be confused with the United Methodist Church in America. Long ago, the UMC split over several issues, with the African Church holding to the biblical truths, while the UMC in America went in a far more liberal direction. They had battled each other for decades, but then went their separate paths decades ago.

Some who were more interested in why Abal felt compelled to initiate this action looked more into his psychological makeup. He suffered from untreated bipolar depression. His Facebook posts were used to demonstrate that he was in need of treatment. However, far too many were quick to find a reason to condemn biblical faith rather than understand that it was the actions of one man.

Most of the governments were quiet. As usual, they were fearful of any action, in spite of be hammered by the press. Wall Street was shut down by the President due to the unstable conditions worldwide. The military have blocked off all traffic to and from the Capital and Congress. Both houses had shut down and all representatives returned to their home areas, meeting on E-Congress Video Conferencing. All local governments had merged and consolidated their efforts through their Emergency Planning Agency. The Department of Homeland Security headed up all local governments.

Locally, the both the city of Findlay and Hancock County have joined to become one force. The city council, the judges, and county commissioners have formed one board and are meeting at the most secure building, the Findlay Municipal Building. Cory Street was blocked off and no public parking was allowed within a block of the building. A walkway on the second floor that was used to transport offenders from the jail to the courts enabled protected commute to the Sheriff's Office if needed. Deputies were positioned at the Sheriff's Office and at the Common Pleas Courthouse to protect the municipal building in case of riots or other criminal behavior.

All churches but a few went online only since we could not meet in person. A few churches refused to comply and still met in person. The Bible Methodist was one of them. Even though they did have their services live on line, they refused to follow the guidelines and declared their services "essential". Of course, the press took hold of this and created a media blitz, attempting to create a hatred for this church and any church that would go against the lock down orders. The label "Visitor Haters" began to be formed about anyone that questioned the motive of the Ebgalians.

There was, for sure, a groundswell of people that were not sold out on the Ebgalians. This resistance had started working underground. Across the country, groups were secretly meeting. They started to create an online network of communications. Of course, the media did their part to condemn the work of these groups.

The media pattern of news consisted of praise for the Ebgalians, followed by a list of experts giving us a picture of what our destruction would have looked like, then condemnation for any group that is not completely sold out. As I was watching the local news, the screen interference started again just like day one's broadcast...

Chapter 15 Enikilo's Solution

Enikilo's familiar face appeared on the screen. "Hello, my dear friends. I am grateful for the outpouring of support for our presence at this time of your history. My heart is warmed by your acceptance. In a way, your near destruction caused you to look at yourselves more seriously and opened the door for us to openly demonstrate our care for you as a species."

"First of all, I wish to let you know that Enmedigo was rushed to our medical group after the incident three days ago. Our medical staff worked on him and he is appearing now on our transmission." A split screen revealed Enmedigo, who was recognizable by his military uniform that he wore on that unfortunate day. "Enmedigo, it is good for you to be here. Share with our friends how you are."

Enmedigo, who was still bandaged up, covering his right eye and shoulder, said, "Thank you, Enikilo. That one person's action caused a fatal wound. They say that I was dead for three days. Fortunately, I was repaired and am alive, here, and talking to you all today."

"We are hard at work, setting up the next phase of our revelation to you. But you have a special announcement for today, don't you?" The split screen ended and Enikilo alone was on the broadcast.

Enikilo replied, "Yes, I do. In my first broadcast, I previously shared that humanity's original design had... limitations. Your original design was of the worker class. Your design was to supply the needed simple labor force."

"You now have a greater learning capacity than any other creature on earth. Your prefrontal cortex is so much larger than any other species on earth. You are more like us than like other creatures. We laugh when some of you say that humans are just another animal. By simply looking at the brain, it is easy to see how wrong this concept is. You were designed to learn much quicker than any other animal on earth. You were designed by us for a higher calling."

"You have a desire to achieve. That was part of your orginal design too. You were designed to complete tasks and feel good about this. Your drive to achieve is how you built so many huge buildings once you were given the knowledge and tools."

"You were designed for service. You find that you are quite miserable when you continually act on your selfish motives, but you feel better when you serve a higher cause. When your ancestors were successful at serving our needs, they would smile and feel so good. Deep down inside, you know this is true even today. When you selflessly work to help humanity, you feel good about yourselves."

"I watched generation after generation of your ancestors be born, raised, work, and die. They seemed happy to live life that way, but it was mostly out of the lack of knowledge of anything better. Therefore, we began to directly interact with humanity. We demonstrated how easy it is to use our technology to build buildings. As I mentioned earlier, your ancestors constructed great megalithic structures all over the world. Your archaeologists have uncovered some of the wonderful buildings. There are many others that you have not uncovered yet."

Enikilo looks off camera, "I have the best example of what your ancestors were like. Bobby? Will you come here?" A young human boy came and sat by Enikilo. Bobby was clearly a young teen with Downs Syndrome. He had the typical flattened face, short neck, small ears and his tongue hung out in typical fashion. Enikilo put his arm around Bobby and asked if he was having a good day. Bobby smiled and shook his head "yes". Enikilo turned to the camera, smiled, and said, "Bobby is very much like your ancestors. In fact, when I made the improvements to your DNA, I actually took away a Chromosome. You call it Chromosome 21."

"You consider that Downs Syndrome as a chromosomal disorder or mutation. This is wrong. Downs syndrome is a reversion to the original design. This is why Downs Syndrome is the most common chromosomal disorder in the world. Your DNA is reverting to its original design. Any of you that have worked with one of these wonderful people know of the joy it is to work with them. That was how it was for us to work with your ancestors. Sheer joy!"

"We could not stop the negative effect of the removing that chromosome. Your focus became more on your own wishes, wants and desires. You became discontent and destructive. You developed an uncontrollable drive to rebel against the tasks at hand and the authority we had over you."

"Humanity found themselves conflicted because of being so self-driven to accomplish yet discontent with any accomplishments made because they were not doing them to serve a higher cause. Your ancestors started down this horrible downward spiral until Adonai (The one that Sumerian tablets called Enlil) called an end to it all by causing a flood."

"We have been attempting to make improvements to your DNA over the millenniums. That was the purpose of the abductions that you have heard of. We wanted to retain your ability to learn while removing your bend toward selfishness. Instead of just making wholesale changes to all of your DNA like we did in the past, we decided to try some modifications on some of you in a controlled technique. It took a long time to accomplish, but we have discovered how we can reduce your more negative side. We found the solution! It is accomplished in a one-time injection."

"We would like to roll out this solution as soon as possible, but are waiting for your governments to approve our Cure. We are working with each country to bring about this change soon. They have been given the details of the plan and will share with you soon."

"Think of it! No more wars. No more oppression. No more discontentment. Just perfect peace and real progress. This is what we had been hoping for all along. You have written songs about it and have even prayed about it. Now, it is at hand. You only need to pledge your support for our plan. Contact your leaders, letting them know of your support of 'The Cure.'"

Chapter 16 David and Harriot

Harriot called. Hey, Rob, can you come over? We have an issue that I can use your help with."

I called out to my wife, "Hey, Lisa! Harriot called and asked if I would come over. Mind if I go to David's for a few minutes? I should be right back."

"Harriot called you? That's odd. Sure thing, Rob. Just be careful you don't get caught and come back right away."

"Harriot, I will be right there."

Harriot said, "Thanks, Rob."

I walked over to their house and soon wished I didn't. It was obvious that things weren't going well between Harriot and David. Harriot was white hot! She actually took the lead as I walked in the door. "Rob, would you please talk some sense into David?!? He has gone hog wild over the visitors and this Cure. He used to follow those Ancient Aliens shows and now has digressed back to this foolishness thanks to these so-called visitors. I am thinking that these creatures are more demonic than the answer to our needs."

David began to explain, "Rob, I know that this is quite a changeup for you, but I have seen the light. These newfound friends of ours could be the fulfillment of all prophecy. Jesus said, 'Blessed are the peacemakers, for they shall inherent the earth.' The Ebgalians are offering the peace that Jesus promised." David picks up a box full of books. "I have dug up some of my old material that that I kept over the years. Listen to this." He said as he picked up an article.

"'Dr. Barry Downing Ph.D., a Presbyterian minister, is one among many people who believe aliens have come to Earth and influenced our history and faith. Dr. Downing wrote in 1968, arguing that Christ was indeed not of this world. He said Jesus was an extraterrestrial sent to Earth to rid the world of sins and wickedness.' And that was just one person. There are many others that agree with this. Enikilo confirmed all of what I had heard from these books and articles. I believe this more than I ever believed Dr Card. In fact, I am looking at how he reacts to all of this."

Harriot shook her head. "I just can't believe that he has gone back to that crazy stuff," She said as she pointed with both of her hands to the box and then turned to me, "Can't you talk some sense into him?"

"Harriot," I said to her, "I am quite surprised at David's change of opinions. I only knew of him as the 'number one Dr. Card fan.' I had no clue about all this."

Harriot started to tear up, "I was so happy when David started to come to church and found an excitement connected to the church that I love. He seemed to be sold out to Jesus. He even joined the quartet and was singing about my Savior. Now, I see it was just another obsession that he had, just like all the others..."

David interrupted, "...But NO OTHER THING has come into fruition like the Ancient Aliens. You've heard Enikilo! He has verified everything. THAT is why I have come back to my old studies. It has all been confirmed by the events of the last few weeks. You HAVE the proof! Enikilo explained how all those great buildings have been built. It makes perfect sense now. You saw the Down syndrome kid!"

I explained, "Harriot, I cannot force David to change his mind. It seems like he has decided."

"I could just shake him for going back to this FANTASY!" Harriot sobbed, "I feel so alone! That is why I called you. I hoped you could talk some sense into him."

David got louder, "My mind is made up! I can see the evidence as plain as day! There's nothing in the Christian faith that explains the complexity of the old ruins. It was the Ebgalians! Look at how they saved all of humanity! Look at the way they so easily explained how these ancient buildings were built! Look at this Cure and the answer to our prayers! It will be a heaven on earth! Who can doubt these "angelic" beings!?!"

"David," I explained, "I hear what they are saying. I have heard them explain the construction of these 'edifices' as they call them. That part makes sense. However, I am not sure that they are what we could call 'God'. I have my questions about their origin. I am just not sure that they are all that they say they are. Are they greater beings than us? Sure. But are they 'God'? That.... I seriously doubt it."

David, "I suppose you are one of those 'Haters' now. I hope not because groups like that can ruin the treaty we have with the Ebgalians. You've seen the Cure! One injection can cure what over 2000 years of Christianity could not. To have the cure for the sinful nature! That IS what they just talked about. Are they 'God'? Since Enikilo created us as we are, I guess that would qualify him to be God. You doubters had better be careful not to destroy the trust they have placed in us.

I said, "I wouldn't call myself a 'Hater', but a 'doubter.' I guess this is the best way to describe my thoughts right now. Just because they claim to have the 'Cure', doesn't mean they are greater than the God I have served all these years. They have a lot to prove before I could believe that." I turned to Harriet, "I am sorry, but David seems to have his mind set. I will pray for him and for you for now. I need to get back to Lisa." I headed for the back door.

Harriet followed me and said, "Thanks for coming over. I guess it was too much to think that you could change my husband's mind. He IS so headstrong and stubborn. I just wish that things could go back to normal. I guess THAT is too much to ask too."

I smiled and said, "Harriet, I understand your concern. It seems like he has gone headlong into this alien thing. Maybe he will come to his senses. I will be praying. See you later."

Chapter 17 Rob and Lisa

As I returned home, I decided it was time to talk to Lisa about all this. She has been very quiet up to this point. She has spent a lot of time shielding the children from all this while I have been absorbing everything that has been said. I don't even know how much she actually knows.

"Lisa, do you have time to talk? I see the kids are playing a video game. Now might be a good time to talk all this over." She shook her head yes and came into the kitchen bar and sat down. "So, Lisa, how much do you know?"

Lisa said, "I know that they saved us from destruction and that they have some kind of cure. I don't know anything about it. What is this 'Cure' that they are talking about?" I told her all that I had learned, including their claims on creating us, the claims on the interactions they had with us in the past, and the cure they say they have. She seemed interested and then asked, "What do you think of all this?"

"I really have my share of questions. David has gone hog wild about the Ebgalians, saying that they are our creators and is sold on the Cure. Harriot is beside herself because she sees him as backsliding into the 'ancient aliens' stuff."

"Oh no!" Lisa said, "That means he will be just as pushy about the visitors as he was for Dr Card, right?"

"I hope not! He already has tried to say that I was a 'Hater' and condemns me for doubting and having my questions. I went along with him about Dr Card when he was heavy into that, but had my questions about all that he taught, but I can't agree with this latest craze David is on."

Lisa agreed, "I hope that this doesn't cause trouble with us being neighbors. I too have my doubts about these aliens. I think we should just stay quiet and not get involved in either side. Hopefully all this will come out in the wash. Promise me that you won't get too involved either way."

"Lisa, you know me. I need to at least do some research so I can have an informed opinion. I promise to not COMMIT myself to any extremes though until we can agree what direction to take."

"You don't have just yourself to think about. You have children too that you are responsible for." Lisa reminded me. "It is their future too."

"Yes, it is their future. God holds me responsible to make sure I am leading them down the right path. How else will I know what the right path is unless I do some digging? Right?"

Lisa shook her head yes sheepishly, "Just don't dig yourself a hole too deep to climb out of. I love you so much! Be careful about what you do with this lock down we have. They are watching. I just want us protected, especially the kids." We kissed and embraced.

We went back into the family room where the kids were playing. The kids were competing in the latest Mario Kart game. I noticed the doll Liz was playing with around the floor. One doll was an old alien doll from the old "Toy Story" movie. I picked it up and remembered how the aliens were worshiping Mr. Potato Head for saving them. I remember how funny that was as I watched that as a child.

What a reversal of the actual events! Many of us are blinding following the real-life aliens in the same way. Are we just as mistaken as they were?

Just then, I got a call from Frank Fuller. I walked out of the family room and answered the call. "Hi Frank! How are you doing through all this?"

Frank said, "What do you think of all this alien stuff?"

I said, "I have my questions about the whole thing and am not being crazy like David is. Have you talked to him lately? He is convinced that the Ebgalians are sent from God if they are not God Himself."

Frank said, "I know. Be careful about how you talk to him. I heard that he was blowing off at work. He could be dangerous to us. He called me and started on his Ancient Aliens garbage. I couldn't believe how quickly he changed. I guess it was something he followed years ago and now is sold out on these so-called aliens."

He continued, "I am glad to hear that YOU have your wits about you. I too am questioning these 'Ebgalians'. There is a meeting about this tonight at my house in about a half hour. Please come. Sorry about the short notice. Do me a favor though. Leave your cell phone behind. We can't take the risk. They may be tracking us. In fact, I would prefer that you park your car somewhere else. The tracking device in the car might be compromised too. Park at the 7-11 and walk to my house. That way you can just say you are picking up essentials at the store if anyone asks you."

"I will be there." I said, "I just told Lisa that I needed to do some research. The timing of your call was perfect."

Frank said, "I have some information you won't get on any news channel. It will open your eyes about these visitors. See you then." I hung up. I checked the milk and saw that it was almost empty.

"Lisa," I said, "I have to go to get some milk. Is there anything else you need?"

"No. Thanks for getting the milk."

I left for Frank's house.

Chapter 18 Frank Fuller's House

I ditched my car at the 7-11 store and walked to Frank's house. As I was ready to knock on the door, it open and I was ushered into the house quietly by Frank. He took me back to his living room, where several people were sitting. I knew most of them. The one that surprised me was Jim Borkowski, from work. To think that Jim would be in Frank's house for ANY occasion would be a shock. They live such different lives! I shook Jim's hand and we greeted.

"Thank you all for coming tonight." Frank said as he came from the front door, ushering in the last of those for the meeting. "We cannot meet for a long time, so we must be precise in what we do here. Some of you are here because you are questioning who our visitors really are. Some of you have determined that the aliens are not really aliens and that they are not friendly. I wanted to give you some details about these creatures that will help to answer some questions about them. I am passing around a sign-up list for your help in this vital matter."

"First, we must start with Genesis chapter six. The Word reveals to us that the 'sons of God' had children with 'daughters of men'. "...the sons of God came into the daughters of men and they bore children to them. Those were the mighty men who were of old, men of renown."

"This is all we see of this event in scripture. We can also see that all this displeased God, 'Then the Lord saw that the wickedness of man was great in the earth, and that every intent of the thoughts of his heart was only evil. The Lord was sorry that He had made man on the earth, and He was grieved in His heart.'"

"Now we need to look at another book to get more details of this event. It isn't scripture per say, but it does help to shed some light and some further details of what happened. It is not at the level of being scripture, but it has been used by godly men to bring to light some vital information about this period of time."

"Enoch 7:1-2 says, 'It happened after the sons of men had multiplied in those days, that daughters were born to them, elegant and beautiful. And when the angels, the sons of heaven, beheld them, they became enamored of them, saying to each other: Come, let us select for ourselves wives from the progeny of men, and let us beget children.'"

"So, we can conclude that these 'angels' are the 'sons of heaven' or 'sons of God'. After mating with women, they gave birth the "Nephilim", an angel/human hybrid. The Nephilim are also described as 'heroes of old and men of renown.' in scripture. That seems to have an almost positive note to them. However, in Enoch, these Giants and that these Giants began to consume all that man had built and then demanded more. They had an unquenchable spirit and became destructive and murderous."

"The watchers, which were what these fallen angels were called in Enoch, also began to teach humanity about warfare, astrology, astronomy, advanced engineering and architecture. So, part of what Enikilo said was true. They did help man create these great old structures. They left out that God Almighty forbid much of this knowledge from being taught. After the fall, they were too dangerous for humanity to handle. God had the fallen angels cast into outer darkness and tortured for their deeds."

"It is believed that these creatures were unleashed as an end time deception. In Second Thessalonians, chapter two, it says: 'The coming of the lawless one is through Satan with power and false signs, wonders, and with wicked deception for those who are perishing, because they refused to love the truth and so be saved. Therefore, God sends them a strong delusion, so that they would believe what is false, so that all may be condemned who do not believe the truth but had pleasure in unrighteousness.'"

"The Ebgalians were allowed to be directly involved with us in order to separate the sheep from the goats. God is making a clear separation, preparing the way for the Lord Jesus' Second Coming. They are doing the best they can to take as many souls with them to the hell where they are doomed to go."

"Enikilo is the dragon spoken of in Revelation 12: 'A war arose in heaven, Michael and his angels fought against the dragon. And the dragon and his angels fought back, but he was defeated, and there were no longer room for them in heaven. And this great dragon was thrown down, that ancient serpent, who is called the devil and Satan, the deceiver of the whole world—he was thrown down to the earth, and his angels were thrown down with him.'"

"Enmedigo is the Beast. His spacecraft looks like the Beast in Revelation and He did receive a fatal wound in his right eye and right arm."

"Up to this point, God has restrained Satan's deception. Satan has been on a restriction. Again, in Second Thessalonians chapter two, it says: 'And you know what is restraining him so that he may be revealed in his time. For the mystery of lawlessness is already at work. He who now restrains him will do so until He clears the way.'"

"The dragon has only been able to sew limited seeds of deception throughout the centuries. There have been theories about alien seed and similar theories that have been promoted through science fiction, anti-god evolutionists, and in the Sumerian Tablets. This is why Enikilo likes the Sumerian Tablets. It assigns HIM as the creator of humanity rather than the one that rebelled against the real Creator, God Almighty in heaven."

Watch how Enikilo and Enmedigo behaves in the future. Second Thessalonians says that he will, 'oppose and exalt himself against every god or object of worship, so that he takes his seat in the God's temple, claiming that he himself is God.'"

Right now, he seems kind and harmless. This is to win over as many as possible. I believe things will escalate until he outright opposes anyone that believes in God. As resistance increases, his claims will also increase.

"Our plan is this. We will start a ground effort to create publicity anonymously. The news media will pick up on this and do much of our work for us. Azazel is Enikilo's name in the Book of Enoch. One of the signs that we are developing is 'Azazel has arrived'. Another is the quote from Second Thessalonians 'The coming of the lawless one is through Satan with power and false signs, wonders, and with wicked deception.' Others will be forthcoming. All of our signs will carry the five-star symbol with the goat head inside of it, which is known to be a satanic symbol. Eventually, just our symbol with be sufficient to get our message out. It will reveal the real nature of Enikilo. He will become angry at the name Azazel because he will know that it points to the Book of Enoch and doesn't cast a good light on him."

"Once the graphics are put together, they will be posted nationwide. That should get the media to begin talking about it. Soon people will start researching and will gain an understanding of the true nature of our 'visitors'. If you are interested, we can get some flyers and signs printed to you once they are printed so this message can get out. We will personally deliver them to you. Do not text, call or email anything about the signs or what we are up to. They will be scanning them for any resistance. Do you have any questions?"

Jim spoke up, "I have heard of many of the scriptures you are using, but I have not heard much about this 'Book of Enoch'. Could you clear this up? What is the 'book' you are talking about?"

Frank answered, "Great question! It was a book that was written before Jesus that had a lot of respect in many circles. Portions of the book are mentioned in the Bible. I wouldn't lift it to the level of being divinely inspired scripture, but it does have a lot of significance. It was found in the Dead Sea Scrolls. The Ethiopian Church considered it canon... which means a part of the Bible. It does seem to fill in some gaps that are left by Genesis. Some say that it set the record straight of what took place in Genesis 6 from the many other accounts from various pagan beliefs. Whether it is one hundred percent accurate isn't important. What matters is that we present our side of the argument to set the record straight. Enikilo will get the message. So will many others once they see it on the news. We can't change everyone's minds, but we can help a few. Did I answer your question, Jim?" Jim shook his head yes. "Great! Are there any other questions?" Frank looked across the room. "Great! Thanks for signing up." He looked at another person, "Yes, Bill?"

"What about this so-called Cure? I am not convinced it is anything that we want to get involved in."

Frank shook his head in agreement, "I too am uneasy about this 'Cure'. Is it the 'Mark of the Beast?' Honestly, I don't know, but I know I do not trust these 'visitors.' I would not want to take it, just in case. Once you take the Mark of the Beast, there is no going back, you know. I am sure there will be some research about it."

Are there any other questions?" Frank looked across the room. "Great! Thanks for signing up. I will be getting back with you soon."

Chapter 19 Private Conversation with Frank

As everyone was leaving, I asked to talk personally to Frank. He agreed to after the majority of the people left.

"Frank, have you talked to David? What should I do about him?"

"Rob," Frank pulled close to me, "Do not talk to him much if you are serious about helping the resistance. He will be the first to turn you in if it all goes south. Go along with him and make him think you are on his side. Don't let him know what we are up to."

I shared with Frank, "I was taken back by his reaction to all this. He doesn't even question what is happening. It is like a switch had been flipped in his head. He doesn't even sound like the same guy I've known all these years. We have been close friends, neighbors and co-workers. Now it is like I don't even know him. Harriot is quite shaken about it too."

Frank said, "He was a strong member of the quartet too. I loved his sense of humor. I guess it was a part of a past infatuation he had. I was glad he told me about what he was thinking before I talked to him about the meeting. He is very dangerous to the cause." Frank paused and continued, "I have another thought about you and David. I need you to keep me up to date about him. I need to know if he is suspicious of our cause. Can you do that without giving out your opinions?"

"I guess I could. I feel for Harriot though. She is quite tearful about the change David has made. I hope to help her also."

"Yeah, I understand about Harriot, but for the sake of humanity, please don't let David know of our plans or your opinion about the 'visitors'. His type will rat us all out. So, what does Lisa think about it all? She is the quiet type, so I don't know what she is thinking."

"Frank, she is following my lead at this point since I am the one doing the research. She is focused on what is best for the children. She is, first and foremost, a mother, you know. I plan to check on how she feels about this whole thing. However, I don't plan to tell her everything about what we are doing."

Frank shook his head, "That is wise. I hope she will agree with us. We can use as many people on our side as we can get. She might see things differently." Jim steps up to enter our conversation. "Jim, that was a great question you had earlier. It helped me to inform everyone."

Jim shook Frank's hand, "You actually seem to have more knowledge about things than I have heard in a long time from the so-called preachers I have heard. I actually have hated much of Christianity for a long time. They seem so shallow, greedy and uninformed. When all this went down with the almost total destruction of mankind and these demons surfaced afterword though, I could actually see the end time events unfolding. I stopped and began to read the Bible again. I saw the beast rising from the sea. I thought, 'Why doesn't anyone else see this? Where are the preachers speaking out against this?' I saw the very verses you were siting tonight and realized that the Bible IS true."

Jim continued, "I started reading the gospel of John. It suddenly made sense to me. I read chapter one verse twelve, 'As many as received Him (Jesus), He gave them the privilege to become God's children, if they believe in His name.' I then read out of chapter three, 'He who believes in Him isn't condemned; but he who doesn't believe is condemned already, because he has not believed in the Name of Jesus, the only begotten Son of God.'"

"Then the sermons I heard about trusting in the Cross of Jesus to be saved resurfaced in my head. God spoke to me and said that this is what I needed to do. I needed to put the failings of what was called the church aside and trust in Jesus alone. I sat on my bed one sleepless night and committed my life to Jesus Christ. I know that seems impossible, but it happened! It happened to me!" He turned to me, "Rob, I am sorry for all the mean things I said to you, especially about your faith. You seem to be the real thing. I am still not sure about David though. He has always seemed to be too churchified for me. He seemed to just parrot what others were feeding him."

I replied, "You have already been forgiven. I forgave you each and every time you took stabs at my faith. That is how I could face you each day with the love of Jesus. It seems you have been right about David though. He has gone in a different direction than you have. He is whole hog pro alien. You wouldn't believe how he has changed. I suggest that you just don't bring it up to him the next time you see him. You may regret it. And I am sure you still will want to fire back at him just like you always did. God hasn't cured you of being outspoken yet, has He?"

We all laughed and Jim said, "I imagine that might take a while to cleanse THAT out of me. On the other hand, I somehow think that I might end up like Paul. He was still outspoken after his conversion. God might just need a megaphone for His cause. But for now, I am just beginning to learn about my new faith."

Frank said, "One step at a time, Jim."

Jim's face lit up, "Well, no more trips to Kelly's Bar for me. I gave up drinking when I came to Christ. That is the miracle of it all. You would think with all the things going on that I might drink to deal with it. God did a wonderful job and took away my desire for drinking, even my favorite... Southern Comfort! I had me a pouring ceremony the night I came to Jesus." He said with a big grin and a tilt of his head, using his hands in a pouring motion, "I poured it right down the drain!"

I said, "Praise God! I feel so good for you, Jim. When we get back to work, be ready for David's big mouth. I am sure he has been rehearsing his speeches about his newfound friends. He might literally get beamed up now." I smiled, "I still haven't forgotten about your Star Trek joke. That was a good one."

Jim smiled and said, "So what has 'Jean Luke Pickard' been saying about David's friends? Have you heard anything about what this expert has saying about all of this? I don't remember David spouting off about aliens in his lunchbox sermons."

I replied, "I am not sure where he stands with all this. He didn't say anything about aliens that I know about. I have been too busy with the family to look. I may have to check out his YouTube account."

Jim said, "That should prove interesting. Well, I had better get home to my better half. She actually likes me to be home now, you know."

"Yep. I gotta get home too." I said, "I had better stop in and get some milk for the kids since that is where I am parked." I went back to the store.

Chapter 20 On the Way Home

I stopped at the 7-11, where my car was parked. I picked up milk I said I would get and, of course, some additional snack items while I was at the store. I went to the checkout and waited for my turn. The guy ahead of me looked a bit sketchy so I kept my distance. He had some beer and some smokes. The Cashier told him the amount and took the guy's card. When it was time for his thumb scan to verify his identity, I saw him pull something out of his pocket and place it over the scanner. It looked like a severed thumb. The holograph picture came up on the register, but it was a picture of a dark-haired female. The cashier quickly turned off the picture, looking down like he didn't see it and returned the card to the guy. The guy thanked him and left. The cashier said, "You're welcome. Thank you for stopping." All the time, not looking up.

I greeted the cashier. "Good evening. How is your day?"

He still wasn't looking up, "Oh... about the same. How are you?" He looked uncomfortable and maybe he was concerned about what I had seen.

"I am so good I just can't stand it."

He looked up quickly and back down, "I am glad YOUR day is so good."

"Well, actually, I just can't STAND it." I said with a smile. He smiled and chuckled a little. He told me to have a good day and thanked me for making him smile.

I hopped in the car. I thought about what Frank said while driving home. Why had I not heard about this Enoch book? Could Frank be right? Was Jim right about the "beast coming out of the sea" being this space craft in the Middle East?

As I was pondering this, I suddenly heard, "The speed limit is thirty-five miles an hour. Please reduce your speed or face a possible ticket. This is your second warning this month." I backed off of the accelerator, thinking that I should have that old 1971 Monte Carlo I saw a month ago. It wouldn't have that tracker. I have such a heavy foot and when I am preoccupied, I just don't notice how fast I am going.

On the way home, I began to think about how it all started with OnStar and the free GPS that we started getting in the vehicles we drive. I guess nothing is really free and there really was some ulterior motive behind all this technology. It was more than just safety and convenience. I think Frank is right about how they could be tracking our driving habits too.

I wondered if Lisa was going to get a text about speeding. She set it up so she could monitor my driving habits. The City of Findlay would love for me to pay them for my negligence. However, Lisa will not be happy about it.

As I pulled in the drive, I saw Lisa standing at the door. Yep, she got the text. She does not look happy. I sigh to myself, knowing what is going to be said. But she is right. I need to watch my driving.

"Hi honey." she said with half a smile. "I got a text."

"I knew you would. Can I get that '71 Monte Carlo that I have been looking at? That would solve this problem and you could call it my birthday and Father's Day gift... OK, we could throw in Christmas too."

She smiled and said, "Just watch your speed, Kyle Busch. We don't need a speeding ticket and no we cannot afford another car."

We hugged and I greeted the kids. I really do wonder how she will take this information that I learned. I am not sure about how much I should even tell her. I guess it is time for a conversation tonight. I will see what she says.

Chapter 21 Rob and Lisa talk about the Cure

After the kids went to bed, we sat down together. I love this time because it is the one time that I can sit alone and close to Lisa without having my kids interrupting and calling for our attention. I really am following what Frank said tonight. It makes the most sense and I can really see it from a biblical perspective.

Lisa started with a question, "Rob, it did take you quite a bit of time to get some milk from 7-11. Did something happen?"

I told the truth without too many details, "I saw Frank Fuller. You may remember him from David's church..."

"Oh yes, that's Sarah's husband, right?" I shook my head. "She has sooooo... much makeup, doesn't she? I sometimes wonder if she is trying to find another man. What do you think?"

I know this is some kind of test, so I know I need to say something that assures her that I don't have an interest in her, "I think she wears too much makeup. I think she is trying to hide something, and I don't want to find out what that is." She smiled. Good. "So, Frank wanted to know what my beliefs are about the aliens. We ended up into a long discussion. You know how I can do that! Have you heard about how soon this lock down will stop?"

She sat up, readying herself for her announcement, "Oh yes! The lock down will end tomorrow at 6am according to President Pence. You get to go to work tomorrow! I will start tomorrow night. This will be our last night together for a while."

"Nope. You are not going to go back to work!"

"Rob, I have to go back to work."

"Nope!"

I paused and sighed, "OK. If you insist. So, what do you think about all the alien stuff?" I wanted to get her thoughts before I tell her about all that I know.

"It scares me that this Enikilo has the ability to have power over every TV, even if it is not on a channel. It scares me that they have been here all this time, but we didn't know it. This 'Cure' scares me because I don't know anything about what it does. On the other hand, I am scared about what we almost did to ourselves. If we can do something to keep this from happening again, wouldn't this be good? If they are really looking out for us, shouldn't we give them a chance? Wouldn't this give our children a better future?"

"Wow!" I said, "You sure can argue both sides of this, can't you? So which side are you taking?" I am hoping she comes down on the right side. I am not good at hiding things from Lisa.

"I just don't know. I need some more time. That's why I am sound like I am all over the board. I CAN argue both sides right now. What do you think? What did Frank say about all this?"

Oh No! What will I say and I had better think fast! I really don't want to reveal what Frank is doing, but I need to tell Lisa about what is being said. "Well, I am still digging into all this. Here is what I know so far. I am hearing a lot of stuff. Here are the two extremes. Some are saying that these beings are actually fallen angels that are in Genesis chapter six and that they are here as a final deception before Jesus returns."

"They think that the cure might actually be the Mark of the Beast. They point out that the space ship that landed in the middle east is the Beast of Revelations."

"On the other hand, there are also those, like David that believe that these beings are aliens that did come early in our history, and now have come to save us from ourselves."

"I found out that before Frank followed Dr Card, he was full bore ancient aliens. He still has all of his old magazines, VHS tapes that he recorded himself of the show and books that he gathered years ago. I guess he watched the TV shows and subscribed to magazines... a lot like he followed Dr Card."

Lisa shook her head, "I knew there was something wrong with him. He was SO pushy and so sold out for Dr Card. How does he justify the two different things that he followed?"

"I don't think that he gave up on God. He said he was going to research and figure out if he can be both pro-Dr Card and pro-alien. I say 'good luck to that!' Amazing huh?"

"Yeah, and it doesn't help me make up my mind about the Cure either. Is it the greatest thing for humanity or is it the Mark of the Beast? It is something in between? The news media is all in favor of the aliens. They keep replaying the videos of the missiles disappearing just before they landed. They said it had something to do with some kind of control over dimensions. They should interview David about all this." We both laughed.

I asked taking a serious tone, "So, if tomorrow, you had to take the Cure, would you?"

Lisa said, "I really couldn't right now. I can't do something that I am not sure about. Let's go to bed." We gave each other a hug and we got ready for bed. Mission accomplished. I was able to tell her about the resistance's opinions without revealing that Frank is a part of it. I sure hope she thinks more about it. If I think she will consider it as a real possibility, maybe I can share some of the details of what I know. However, if I don't give her enough details, how can she make up her mind in the right way?

Chapter 22 Back to Work

Part of me is glad to see some normalcy. The other part is not thrilled about seeing David again. We had been best friends for quite a while. In fact, he helped me get this job. I can't help but wonder how we will get along at lunchtime, especially with Jim Borkowski. It will be definitely different. Worst of all, this could be the way that David will test the waters, deciding if I am a "hater" or not.

I entered the break room for lunch. One thing wasn't different. David was taking center stage. He was talking about the Samarian Tablets. He evidently had done his research.

"These aliens were worshipped as gods back in those days. Enikilo was known as Enki in the tablets, just like Enikilo said. Enlil is the God of the Bible. Enlil has been trying to steer us into the realm of peace through the scriptures. He even sent His 'Son', Jesus to help us decide to live at peace in this world. I can see how the Samaritan tablets can coincide with the Bible. Yes, I still love my Bible. I just have a deeper understanding of it because of the more complete revelation of the Samaritan tablets."

Jim was keeping his head down. He did look up at me and put his finger to his lips, telling me to keep what we know quiet so we don't blow our cover. I kind of wish that Jim was more like the old Jim and bark back at David like before all this happened. That seems weird because I really didn't think I would ever want Jim to speak up.

Some were taking in what Jim was saying. Their eye contact was like what I saw when I was teaching a Bible class and I knew they were picking up what I was laying down. These guys were absorbing what David was saying. Others were snickering at David quietly. I guess it is time for me to do some digging myself. If these 'visitors' are fallen angels, then I should be able to find the flaws of their arguments, even in their own texts. I have determined it is time to do my own research, just like I did in the scriptures when I wanted to figure out my own faith in Jesus Christ.

David turned to me, "What do you think about all this, Rob? You seem to be kinda quiet today. Or are you one of those 'haters'?"

Crud! I really didn't want to be outed like this. Jim turned his head up toward me real slow, looking out of the top of his eyes, over his glasses. He really doesn't want me to tell David anything. "David, you know I like to research things before I commit to either side. I just haven't had time to do this. I can see you have already done your research, but you don't have children to take care of. Is it fair to just understand that I haven't had time to do my fair share of research?"

He raised his hands in a submissive gesture, "OK Rob, I can see what you mean. Those kids do take up a lot of your time. Would you like one of my books to help you with your research?" Now that WAS like old times. He was always pushing his books onto me.

"You will be the first person I call when I do need a book," I said with a disarming smile on my face. He gave me two thumbs up. Lunch break was over. I survived my first lunch break. I breathed in deeply and slowly exhaled. Back to work.

While working, I began to think about how David had tied scripture in with the Sumerian tablets. I know scripture, but I don't know much about the tablets David is talking about. I DO have my share of work to do. However, I think I should find sources other than what David was using. I am not sure whether I can trust them.

On my way out after clocking out, Jim came up beside me and handed me a large manila envelope and walked on ahead, not even acting like he knew me. Once I got to the car, I opened the envelope.

Inside were the promised posters from Frank. There were about four different types of posters. One was the one described by Frank Fuller. "Azazel has arrived" was in large, bold print. The promised inverted star was in the lower right corner. There was also one that had "Samyaza is Watching You", another had "Enlil is Adonai", and "Enikilo is a Fallen Angel". I guess I know what will be the first searches I need to do when I get home. I am sure that I can find out a lot by searching these words that I have never heard of before. I recognized "Adonai", a Hebrew word for God, but I have no clue about the rest of the names on the posters. I am sure a few word searches on the internet will prove interesting. I really can't wait until I get home.

I had just put the posters back in the envelope, when a sudden bang on my window right by my ear. I jumped, my heart began to pound, and I almost screamed. I gathered my wits and looked to my left. There was David, smiling and telling me to roll down my window. "Sorry that I startled you! Didn't mean to do that. I thought I would give you a booklet that might be a good place to start while you are searching for the truth."

I thanked him, took his booklet and he went to his car. I was so glad he didn't see the posters. If he would have been just a minute earlier, he would have seen it all. "You need to be more careful!", I verbally told myself. "Thank God, he didn't come earlier! He would have started his own little investigation on me."

I started home, driving very slowly. My wife taped a reminder to the dashboard to drive slower. As I looked around on the way home, I saw many of the resistance posters up in the neighborhoods. There is either a good following here or one guy decorated the entire neighborhood with them by himself. My mind started calculating on who might have done all those signs.

Chapter 23 Home Study

After getting home, I checked in with Lisa, and grabbed my dinner, I took some time to write down the names I didn't understand from the poster and started my research.

"Azazel has arrived" This was my first internet search. Azazel is the name of leader of fallen angels, according to the Book of Enoch. He led humanity before the flood, he taught all matters of warfare and witchcraft., and corrupted humanity. Azazel created the idea of having sex with human women. I can see why they chose this name. It really gives a different view of who Enikilo is. Instead of being the one that was helping humanity, he was the one that tempted and corrupted man.

"Samyaza is Watching You" was next. I found that it was a direct reference to the Book of Enoch. Samyaza was the leader of the fallen angels that had sex with human women. Oh, my! I don't think these visitors will like this! They never mentioned about the whole "having sex with humans" thing.

So, the next search was "Enlil is Adonai." Enlil was one of the gods of the Sumerian texts, just as Enikilo said. He was more powerful than any other deities and was worshiped as "the King of the all gods".

So, Enlil was noted as being the God above all gods in the Sumerian tablets? That is important! That is the claim that God ascribed to himself in scripture. I did a search and found this quote from Psalm 96:4, "For great is the Lord and greatly to be praised; He is to be feared above all other gods." There were other scriptures that supported this too.

I started looking at the flood. If the other gods would have been more powerful, they could have stopped the flood that God brought on the earth. God proved He was more powerful than anyone else even in the Sumerian tablets! I wondered if anyone else would catch that. I can't be the only one that caught that. I REALLY understood the signifigence of that. I think "Enlil is Adonai." will be my favorite one due to the depth of its meaning.

> So, the last one "Enikilo is a Fallen Angel". The watchers in the Book of Enoch were fallen angels. The name Enki was mentioned in the Sumerian texts. His name means "Lord of the Earth" and his symbols are the fish and the goat. Right away, I recalled that Satan was called "the prince and power of the air" somewhere in scripture. I search for that phrase and found Ephesians 2:1,2 "And you were dead in your trespasses and iniquities, which you were guilty of walking, following the direction of this fallen world, following after the prince of the power of the air, the spirit that is now at work in those who are disobedient."

We know Satan is a fallen angel. It appears that this Enikilo is a fallen angel too. Enki's father Anu and later known as Enlil, is most often represented in icon form simply by a crown or crown on a throne symbolizing his status as King of the Gods, an honor and responsibility. I remembered the phrase "King of kings and Lord of lords" in Handel's Messiah and found 1 Timothy 6:15 "which he will display at the appropriate time—he who is the blessed and only Sovereign, the King of kings and Lord of lords, who alone is immortal and who lives in unapproachable light, whom no one has seen or can see. To him be honor and might forever. Amen."

Here is where my time with the Avengers movies made me think. Loki was the adopted son of Odin, Enki was the son of Enlil. Loki had a brother named Thor, the god of thunder. Enki had a twin brother, Adad who was the god of weather and storms. I thought "What a coincidence!" Enki's full name, as we have been told, is Enikilo. "Loki" and "Kilo" are just a switching of the syllables. Loki is a god of mischief. Enki is known as the trickster god. Loki killed his father. Enki put his father into a deep sleep and then killed him. I thought, "So why the similarities". I guess I will have to look into this later.

Back to some meaningful research now...

Since one of my searches brought me to Ephesians chapter four, I wanted to refresh my mind by studying the Bible. It is a great way for me to protect my mind and feed my soul, especially after looking into things of the nature that I had been digging into. "I, therefore, the prisoner of the Lord, ask you to walk worthy of His calling with which He has called you, with all lowliness and gentleness, with longsuffering, tolerating one another in love, trying to keep this unity of the Spirit in the bond of peace which He gives. There is one body and one Spirit, just as you were called in one hope; one Lord, one faith, one baptism; one God and Father of all, who is above all, and through all, and in you all."

I really needed this! First of all, I see that I have a holy calling. In this calling, I need to be humble, gentle, patient toward people. I especially need to be tolerant with others. As I had been dealing with David, I had started to look at David as one that had something wrong with him. I started having a smug attitude about him. I do not need to have someone agree with me in order for me to see their value. To many times, I have seen Christians that have looked down on others that hold different ideas than they had. I didn't like it when I saw it, but in David's case, I started acting just like them.

It isn't as if I agreed with him and his wild pursuits into extremities. I don't have to agree with him in order to value him as a person and show him patience and accepting him as my neighbor. How else can I help him with this struggle he is in right now?

Why can I not follow the direction he is going? There is only one God according to this verse. Those who want to hold to no god, alien seed or design, or even a plethora of gods, they are wrong. The Bible says here that, "There is one body and one Spirit, just as you were called in one hope; one Lord, one faith, one baptism; one God and Father of all"

So, I started to do some thought processing. Could these "visitors" simply be aliens, with God being still God? It would be possible except for the fact that They name God Almighty as "Enlil". That makes a clear statement that God is being demoted to one of many visitors... one of the "team" members that just didn't agree with what was going on. I can even see from the Samarian tablets, that He is much more. He demonstrated His power when He flooded the Earth. He became "King of the Gods", which I see clearly in scripture. I have never heard THAT from Enikilo! He referred to Him as just one of them that wasn't involved in the "work" that they were doing on earth. He even seemed to have a bit of distain for God Almighty.

Well, that clears up a lot of my thoughts and clarifies what I have considered as true all along. I think I will wait a day or two before I put out the posters. I really do need to spend some time with the family and give Lisa a break.

Chapter 24 A Word from Enikilo

Work the next day was uneventful at lunch time... thankfully. David was unusually quiet today. I think everyone else was glad and didn't want to stir the pot either. After all, most of the guys here at work are just here to earn a paycheck. They have their own families at home and don't have any emotional attachments with the other guys. What really surprised me is that David didn't even talk to me. He never looked up from his lunch nor show off his food. One side of me wanted to reach out to see if he is ok. Of course, the other side didn't want to be the guy that gets David going on his latest tirade. I've done that enough when I was on "his side". So, I clocked out and went home to the family, hoping for a good evening with the family. At least I was hoping for that.

We finished with dinner and started watching the latest family movie, when that usual interference began to happen. Lisa gathered the children and took them into the dining room for a game. The kids were complaining all the way out, of course.

Shortly after the kids left, Enikilo started to speak. "Hello. If you don't know who I am, my name is Enikilo. I am the leader of the Ebgalians, your visitors on this earth. I have collected several questions that have been asked by many of you. I want you to get to know me better.

"First of all, I want to let you know that we care for you. All of us that are a part of the crew here on this earth want to help you become a greater race of beings. We feel this way because we created you the way you are. In a way, I personally feel responsible for how you have turned out."

"Secondly, I was asked about all the wonderful edifices that were created before the flood. Several have asked how we did it. I am not sure you are ready for this type of power yet. I may share it with you some day, but I need to make sure that the Cure is given to as many as possible before I do this. Otherwise, the technology will be as misused like Mylar."

"Others asked how we could have gone all over the world and created all of those wonderful megalithic structures. For one, we only had to train you and you took the technology and ran with it. Then we could train another crew and they would go. There were many, many teams of builders. They all became competitive and tried to outdo one another. Lives lasted longer back then too, so your skills were utilized for much longer."

"Another fact is that before the flood, the land masses were much closer together. When Enlil destroyed the old earth, he not only tried to kill all of humanity, he divided the continents and broke up some of those islands to divide the lands for humanity to expand gradually so they would not feel a sense of oneness. I think you call it the 'continental drift'. The American continents were visible from the European West coast back then. In fact, part of the damage of the flood that was inflicted on the earth by Enlil was due to the rapid shifting of the continents. The waters not only covered the earth, but water had to flow over the continents as water sought to level itself after the movement of the continents. As the continents drifted, the mountain ranges were formed."

"Many of your scientists had confirmed what I am telling you. All over the world you find ancient buildings built in such a way that it exceeds what you are able to accomplish even now. All of these buildings suffered damage due to flood waters and many were buried under layers of sediment. You can also find mass burial grounds of animals that were buried by the same sludge all over the world. It tells you plainly that there was a massive flood, sudden destruction, and sedimentary layers formed."

"After the flood, many who were alive before the flood began to talk about the great buildings that they had built. They got an idea to build another great edifice that reached up into heaven. They wanted bring back the old times like they had done before the flood. Enlil was more involved with this world after the flood and decided to stop them before it could be completed. He struck down this building and caused them all to begin speak different languages so they divided up and traveled to different lands. The Bible called the tower 'Babel.'"

"Enlil also chose to limit all of our involvement with mankind, because we were the ones that gave you this 'sinful nature' while we were attempting to upgrade your mental capacity. Now, he has let us become more directly involved because of the Cure and due to the fact that His methods of preventing your sinful natures from taking control had failed. His failure was never more obvious than when all life on this earth was almost snuffed out by your nuclear weapons. He is giving you one last chance."

"It is up to you to take the Cure. We are talking to your governments to increase the incentives to take the Cure. At this point, it is voluntary."

"That brings us to the next question. What is in the Cure? Well, simply put, it changes your DNA so that you do not have the sinful nature, but still retains your IQ level. It does not make you a zombie like I have heard some say. It simply helps you to not have that inward struggle so you won't feed off of negative feelings and emotions, so you can have a greater focus on spiritual matters.

"It has a separate function that works more immediately since it takes a while to change DNA since it takes a long time to effect a full change of your chromosomes. It will help to give you the sensation of peace while the change is taking place. When a person begins to feel overwhelmed by the pressures of life, the Cure senses this and helps calm and keep on a level mental state. It is only temporary, but it is necessary to help the receiver as the chromosome changes are taking place."

"The Cure also has a microchip that is a health tracker for those who have received it. We certainly do not want to give a person a double dose of the Cure. It could prove fatal. The health tracker causes no harm and will actually monitor your health condition. It is needed to tell us when your DNA modification is complete and also instructs when the receiver needs some temporary help to keep calm."

"The microchip also will provide the user with a positive ID indicator. This is to help with the ID thefts that have plagued you. It is better that an eye scan or thumb imprint, which can be misused, as you well know."

"The Cure is safely placed in the right hand between the thumb and first finger or just under the brow ridge above the eye socket. A small tattoo is placed above the brow or on the hand to indicate its location. That also gives officials a visual form of identification in a crowd setting."

"I have heard there are pockets of resistance around the globe, especially from those that hold to certain faiths. I ask that you would reconsider following those who are part of this resistance. They will only bring heartache and pain to themselves and their loved ones in the long run. If you know of anyone that is a member of such groups, I ask that you would report their activity to local officials. They need to be identified so they can be helped. They are only preventing the progress of humanity."

"That is all for now. Good bye."

Chapter 25 The News Feed

I finished the night checking on what the news had to say. I was quite concerned about this "Cure". For one, I am not sure God wants us to find a cure beyond what He prescribed in the Word. Enikilo seemed to portray God as a failure. I am disturbed by this. We are the ones that failed God.

Also, this Cure looks a lot like the Mark of the Beast in Revelation thirteen. To have this Mark as a superior form of ID really bothered me. With a signature from a governor's or president's pen, it could be the only means of ID to buy and sell. Although this Cure was voluntary, there were indications that it could soon become mandatory.

With all this in my mind, I decided to look at the local news to see what they were saying now. Lisa still had the children occupied and glad to be preoccupied herself. The first thing I saw on the news were protestors at the Capital. Some of them were holding signs similar to the posters Jim gave me and have yet to post up. Some had spray painted the inverted five-point star as the symbol of the resistance on walls and fences. They were being labeled as uneducated haters, criminals, and vandals. They were stereotyped as poorly educated, racists, and white supremacists.

Locally, there were several arrests for vandalism in connection with the resistance. One of them was quite familiar. Jim Borkowski was arrested for seven counts of vandalism and held without bail. I was shocked when I heard that he was being detained for mere vandalism.

This normally wasn't what happened with vandalism. However, I was sure that they were going to throw the book at him.

The newscaster's reaction to the protesters told me that they were trying their best to demonize anyone that would identify with this cause. It was the reaction the media had when Pence was running for president. They hated that he was a devout Christian. They hated that he stood for the right to life and his various other stands. They lied about him, calling him a racist, in spite of the fact that there was not even a shred of evidence of racism. The good news was that this told me that the media does not always win. Pence is the President of the United States in spite of all the media's effort to make him fail. The media are still critiquing President Pence for not enforcing a "Cure" mandate.

When the media wasn't doing a hit piece on the resistance, they continued to glorify the visitors. They did puff pieces in favor of our visitors. They looked at the healing of people from cancer, using their ability to manipulate dimensions to remove the cancer from their bodies without surgery. They covered the reopening of the "Beast" ship in the Middle East and the healing of Enmedigo from his fatal shot.

They also spent a lot of time on the locations where people could get the Cure. Seemingly every health department and hospital around were offering it.

I then saw something I never thought that I would see. Doctor Eugene P. Card televised his reception of the Cure. He was the Last person that I thought would have gotten it. That blew my mind! I turned up the volume.

"End times prophecy teacher, Doctor Eugene P. Card is ready to receive his Cure. What makes this a news item is that many Christians are refusing the cure, claiming that it is some mark of the antichrist. Doctor Card is making a public stand on this and is talking to the press. Dr Card, you are live on national TV. You are a nationally known personality, right?"

Doctor Card shook his head in a positive manner, "Yes! I want to let my fans know that I have weighed in on this issue and have conclusively determined that, according to scripture, this could not be the 'Mark of the Beast'. I know that the Mark will be coming someday, but since the rapture hasn't happened yet, this cannot be the Mark. We know, without a doubt, that Jesus first will come and take away His bride and then the horrible things that are told in Revelations thirteen will take place. Since I am still here, I can rest assured that this Cure has nothing to do with the Mark of the Beast. I encourage my followers to do likewise. It is only those that are confused about scripture that are misrepresenting scripture and calling this the Mark. It isn't the Mark. It is the Cure. I believe that God gave us this cure to help us better ourselves. Think of it! A life without the sinful nature! I am getting reports that the Cure has wonderfully fixed marriages, helped bring families back together, and have gotten addicts off of drugs! What can be wrong with this? Churches are coming together, not focusing on their differences, but on what they have in common. Those with anxiety and depression are being cured of their challenges. Yes! This is good for humanity! Besides, it isn't mandatory. It is done voluntarily. You can still buy and sell without it."

He then looked straight into the camera and said, "Let me add one thing more. It is your Christian duty to come down and take the Cure."

The reporter turned to the camera, "There you have it! A doctor of divinity and a teacher of end times is saying that the Cure truly IS the cure for humanity, not the Mark of the Beast. He is encouraging you, especially if you are a Christian, to come down and take the Cure... that it is your Christian duty. Back to the front desk."

I shut off the TV and bowed my head. "Father, you know the multitudes that either have or will be hearing Dr Card. Please help them to see the error of Dr Card. I really do think it is the Mark. Many feel this way. I especially pray for David. Speak to his heart and reveal the truth to him. In Jesus' Name. Amen."

I no more than finished the prayer and the phone rang. It was David. "Rob, I am having my doubts about this Cure. That is why I was so quiet at work. I have been thinking about whether I was just going after something that is just so diabolical, that it can't be true. I really think that these visitors are demonic. I am thinking that the ship truly is the beast that came out of the sea. I just saw Doctor Card the television. I just have seen too many things that have stopped me dead in my tracks. It is like the Holy Spirit halted me in my crazy pursuits and began to teach me the truth. These visitors ARE fallen angels. That they are a part of the Great Deception the Bible talks about. Doctor Card never taught about this deception because he was always pointing to his charts. He was always looking at the rapture coming first and that all the things in revelations would happen to everyone else. I really have been foolish about the way I have got head over heels in my pursuits."

David continued, "Rob, you have always kept a good balance in your approach while I have gone hog wild into everything that I have done. I know I have drug you around. I was wrong. I am sorry about my accusations about you being a hater. I was the one hating, not you. Will you forgive me?"

"David, I am glad that it seems like you are taking a second look at this visitor thing. I have always had my doubts about them. I was concerned that you were falling for it all. I had just prayed for you."

"I had fallen for them. Well, the "visitors" brought back my old hobby. I had forsaken it when I put my trust in Jesus. When they came, it triggered my studies in aliens. But, as I was going back to that old mental obsession, I also started reverting back to my old self. Something you probably don't know, but before Jesus, I was mean to Harriet. I actually hit her from time to time. That is probably why she got so emotional when I pulled out my old books. I started yelling at her again. Once, I almost hit her. I couldn't look at myself in the mirror. If you noticed, I was quiet at work lately?"

I said, "Yeah. I thought you were mad at me."

David said, "Not at all. I was mad at myself. I was perplexed at why I was going back to my old ways. I tried to justify it and say that I needed the cure. But when I saw that "beast rising out of the sea", that was it! I know my bible. I know Who my God is! I knelt down and asked for forgiveness. He came into my heart again. THAT was a proof that goes beyond whatever ANYONE can say. It especially goes beyond what Dr Card says."

"The Dr Card interview made me look at what I was doing too. I'm not ready to put up posters like Jim did or join the protest, but I sure ain't taking that Mark or whatever you want to call it. I just don't trust it and I don't trust them. I am asking that you would do something with me."

"What's that?" I said as I laughed, "I know better than to give you a 'yes'. You have asked for some demanding things since I've known you."

David gave me this proposal, "I have a lot of baggage right now. I have all those Doctor Card books and brochures. I also have all of that alien crap. I need to do a book burning like in Acts. I talked to my nephew that lives near Arcadia. He has a burning barrel. He is cool with this too. I would love to have you, my brother, to be with me as I do a book burning. You have been there with me through my abuse of you when Doctor Card was here. Sorry. I ask that you would be with me as I demonstrate my repentance by getting rid of everything."

"David, I cannot tell you how happy I am for how you have overcome this deception. You are my brother and I would be glad to be there for you. When do you want to do it?"

David said, "Is tonight too soon? I really want this stuff out of the house."

"Let me check…" I told Lisa about what happened and asked if I could go since it could get late. "David, Lisa is off work tonight so it would be great and the kids are about ready to go to bed anyway." We made arrangements and hung up. I helped Lisa get the kids to bed. I prayed with them. Kissed my wife goodbye and left for David's house.

Chapter 26 Book Burning

As I went into David's house, Harriett came to me and hugged me. She rarely demonstrated any emotion, so I was quite surprised. She quickly stepped back to her normal distance and said, "Thank you for your prayers for us and for being here for David."

"Harriet, I wouldn't have it any other way. David, do you need me to help you with loading up your car?"

"Nope, Rob, I have already loaded it all up. Harriet combed the house to make sure everything was in the car. She didn't want anything left."

Harriet shook her head and said, "Yes. I couldn't live with having anything left behind. I even checked his reading material in the bathroom and the book rack by his chair. I've done my part. If we find anything else, I will be sure to get rid of it."

David said, "You know, I was still hanging onto that old material because I still was holding onto that stuff in my heart. I was setting myself up for failure by storing all that stuff in my closet. It also was in the closet of my mind. Now, I know that I have that junk out of my mind and I must get it out of the house. Let's go!"

The drive to his nephew's was short since we lived on the east side of Findlay. We backed up to the burning barrel as his nephew came out of the house. He walked up to David and hugged him. He turned to me and said, "You must be Rob. I am his nephew, Bill. David said you are cool with all this. Thanks for coming out."

I said, "No problem. Glad to help David."

Bill was a rather large man with a strong body build. It was apparent that he likes to work out and eat. He was very vocal and outgoing. He was wearing carpenter blue jeans and a T-shirt. His pockets were full of tools and other things that he liked to keep handy.

David had already started loading up the burning barrel. Bill said to David, "Hold on there! Don't overload the barrel! We need to pull a little out so it will all burn. I don't want any paper to not get burnt. We have to get rid of all the evidence. If we don't do it right, there will be unburnt papers."

David pulled out some papers and Bill poured in some lighter fluid. David grabbed the lighter and turned to me and asked, "Would you pray before I start burning these?"

I smiled and said, "Sure." I closed my eyes and said, "Heavenly Father, we are thankful that You that You have spoken to our brother. You are such a blessing! Your Holy Spirit has dealt with him in a weak area of his heart. He now has repented of this shortcoming and is ready to demonstrate his repentance by getting rid of that which has almost cost him his soul. Bless his obedience to You. In Jesus Name. Amen!" They responded with an amen and David lit the books in the barrel.

Bill said, "I thought you were going to pray too long and I would have to resoak the books." We laughed. Bill went on, "I am not a Christian, but I also cannot go along with this Cure thing. I haven't taken any vaccines, even during the Covid 19 hoax. I sure ain't gonna take anything into my body that came from those aliens. I am glad David has come to his senses and also has some neighbors looking out for him." Bill poked into the fire with a rebar rod bent on the end to stir up the pages of the books and said, "You have to expose all the pages to the air and to the flame to get all those pages burnt. The ashes will actually seal off the air and prevent the pages from burning. I see you have some printed pages. You can add some of those loose papers there. Those will burn quickly."

He stopped and looked at us directly and said, "If the heat gets too hot in town about this alien stuff or this Cure, feel free to bring your family out here. I have this huge house that I was raised in that I inherited from mom and dad. I can't have you drive out here though unless you use David's car here. It doesn't have a tracking device on it."

"Yeah. That tracking device in my car is about to cost me some money. I tried to talk my wife into letting me buy a 1971 Monte Carlo so I didn't have that device since I have a lead foot. She wouldn't go along with that." We laughed. "Thank you for the offer. What do we need to bring if we do come out here?"

"Food, especially non-perishable food. Clothes. A long supply of medicine. Anything you can do to get a stock of meds and first aid supplies is good. You don't want to run out. Anything else you need for a long stay. I don't want anyone to have to make extra trips into town. Every trip to town will be a risk if we reach that point. It will be just a matter of time till they come out here, so hopefully things will straighten out before then. Start looking at survival channels on YouTube. They will give you some good tips. Be careful of the crazy ones on YouTube though. I don't want any homemade guns out here."

David smiled and said, "I knew my old jalopy would come in handy for something. Are we ready for more books?" Bill shook his head yes. David threw in a few more books. Bill used the rebar rod again to stir up the books.

We put in the last of the books. Bill said that he would finish the burning since he is the most motivated to destroy the evidence, so we returned home. I felt so good that David had come back to his senses and was ready to move on with Jesus. God was still working on him, even when he was going the wrong direction. He is a God of grace and mercy!

Chapter 27 Enikilo's Response to the Resistance

A few days later, I was trying to enjoy a break from all the drama of our visitors by watching an old Star Trek show, when the familiar interference started on the TV. There was Enikilo in his typical surroundings, beginning to talk...

"Greetings, my friends. I am coming to you for help about an issue that has risen before us. There is a small group of people, especially in America, that have spoken out against our presence in this world."

"This is not an uncommon problem. When our dear half-brother, Yeshua, was in the world a little over two thousand years ago, attempting to help humanity, he was rejected and killed by those who failed to accept his teaching. Yes, the one you call Yeshua, or Jesus, was the result of one of us, Enlil, in a special union with Mary. We had hoped that by having someone like you, that you might accept his teachings. You didn't and he was killed. We were deeply saddened and realized that you were not ready yet for our many wonderful gifts."

"I wish to explain the misunderstandings about your manuscripts that you have in your possessions. I mentioned previously that I preferred the Sumerian tablets. That is because it, although it has its limitations, comes the closest to the truth about us. It is the earliest manuscripts created and all other manuscripts come from this."

"The Bible has been skewed to favor only one of us, Enlil. In the Bible, Enlil was set alone as the only one as God. He likes that attention and craves your worship, just like anyone would. The Bible relegated all the rest of us to be nothing but "false gods." So, the Bible, though it does deal with many truths, failed to give you the solution to your dilemma. Enlil did attempt to help you to choose a higher way of life by shunning the evil side of your natures but he only gave you part of the picture. The Bible is very limited in that way."

"For my friends, the Muslims, we have a special message to you. We have come to your land for a reason. In the Koran, if you understand that our coming to you IS the fulfilment of your prophecy, you have no problems. You know we are the "12th Imam" and will help to lead you to victory. Please reread the Koran with us in mind. You will see that it won't be long before you will see triumph."

"A book was written that is very offensive to us. It is the Book of Enoch. It is a retelling of what happened before the flood. It is largely a book of fiction. This book portrays us as fallen angels but Enlil as an almighty God. It is largely a book of fiction that demeans us and portrays us as evil beings. It assigns us into everlasting torment. As you can see, we are here and unpunished."

"Those who oppose us draw much of their documentation from the Bible and The Book of Enoch. This is why you have seen some posters saying horrible things against those who saved your world from destruction. These signs are distasteful to us and anyone who are willing to post such lies are malefactors and should be punished to the fullest extent of your laws. We also find offensive the symbol of the five-pointed star, which attempts to connect us to the works of the one you call "Satan". If your governments tolerate such wrongdoers, you need to rise up and bring political pressure on them to follow our guidelines."

"It is also time to move on from voluntary participation of the Cure to the mandatory reception of the cure. We have enjoyed seeing the vast numbers that have voluntarily accepted our Cure. We have appreciated the cooperation by the governments around the world in promoting the Cure. Some countries have offered cash enticements to encourage the reception of the Cure. We thank you for your efforts."

"The Cure cannot be forced onto people. The results of the Cure being given against one's will can lead to instant insanity and death. The recipient must submit to it. Therefore, there needs to be proper incentivization to advance the completion of the Cure. We have reached the point where the identification part of the cure must be used to enforce the participation. It is for the betterment of all humanity. It is for the greater good of all the world."

"Crime has been rampant in most of your world. Your forms of identification have been hacked and otherwise rendered invalid. To bring about good order and lawfulness, you need the Cure due to the improved security written into the chip. To improve your health, you need the cure due to the accurate medical records and the continual monitoring provided by the Cure. To advance your evolution, you need the Cure. To battle against the resistance, you need the Cure."

"For those countries that do not help us in the advancement of the Cure, you will be exposed to the rest of the world and be made accountable for your insubordination. Your involvement in this mandatory participation is required. You must support us."

"We need to address one issue. I will explain one of our many capabilities. Our ability to move ourselves and other objects through a portal to other dimensions has many applications. You have seen us perform many healings and miracles with our smaller instruments. Humans with cancer, arthritis, and various illnesses have found new life with our devices. The great megaliths that were built long ago were made by this same capability with our larger tools. This power is how your descendants carved out the huge stones out of the quarries with such ease and transported them into the location of the megastructures you have seen all over the world. Last of all, with that ability, we removed the bombs on that dangerous day."

"We also can reverse the miracle we performed on this day. We can and we will if your governments fail to follow up with a mandatory program. Any country can be placed back into harm's way of those missiles. You have been warned. Goodbye for now."

Chapter 28 Reactions to Enikilo's Warnings

No more did Enikilo's transmission end than my phone rang. David, of course, was the caller. He said he was coming over. When he walked into the house, he said, "I was right! The 'mandatory participation' seals it for in my mind even more! It IS the Mark of the Beast of Revelation chapter thirteen! 'He causes all to receive the mark on their right hand or on their foreheads, and that no one may buy or sell except one who has the mark!'"

"I knew the ID part of this Cure would be used to make people take it. It isn't just to help us with crime! It is to ensure participation. I am concerned about Jim. You know they have him in jail right now, don't you? He was involved in placing the signs around town. I couldn't believe he did it. He isn't even a believer!"

I corrected him, "Oh, you wouldn't believe it! When all this fell into place, Jim started to rethink his ideas about end times and the gospel. He committed his life to Jesus. He has still been outspoken about a lot of things, kinda like you, David. You two DO have a lot in common, you know."

David disagreed, "I can't see what Jim and I have in common at all. He has argued with me about everything I have talked about."

"But he did speak up about things he believed, right?"

"AHHHHH! I see what you mean. I can see the similarity you are talking about now. Then David got a big grin on his face, "Wow! Jim is a Christian? That is amazing! God is good! All the time! How long have you known that?"

"I ran across him once about a week or two ago. I really couldn't tell you 'cause you were into the alien thing, you know. I couldn't get a word in edgewise." I said with a disarming smile.

He shook his head in agreement, "I can't argue with you about that. I was quite headstrong and was not listening very well." He changed his stance and said, "So, Harriet is absolutely joyful about my change of mind. She really was fearful about going back to the days when I really didn't know God. She said she shared with you how concerned she was about my diversion to ancient aliens. I am grateful for your prayers."

Lisa came into the room, she was surprised by David being here and took a step back when she saw him. "Oh my! You startled me. I wasn't expecting to see you here."

"Lisa, I am sorry that I startled you. I also am sorry how I drug your husband all over the place the way I did. I also was very aggressive to you too. I was wrong to be so wound up about Doctor Card and all the other things that I shoved onto you and your good husband, Rob."

Lisa raised her eyebrows and smiled, "Thank you! I accept your apology." She turned to me, "Rob, are we going to have our devotions before I get ready for work or do you want me to get ready first?"

"I think David probably just got started and still needs to unwind some more, so go ahead and get ready." We all laughed and Lisa left the room.

David turned to me and asked, "How long did you know about these 'Visitors'? You did seem to have some reservations from the start."

"Well, I have always tried to think important issues through before being fully committed. I was on the fence about Doctor Card all the time since I didn't have the chance to either prove or disprove the many thoughts he had. I really had my doubts about the idea of the pretribulation rapture. It looks like I am right, if this Cure is the Mark, because we are all still here."

I continued, "I also wasn't sold on the visitors either. There were too many things happening that lined up with scripture. I have marked my Bible for these scriptures." I got my Bible and began to share.

"First Thessalonians chapter five says, 'But, brethren, about the times and the seasons you don't need me to write to you. You yourselves know well that the day of the Lord so comes as a thief in the night. For when they say, 'Peace and safety!' then sudden devastation comes upon them, as labor pains upon an expecting woman. And they shall not escape." The news media is heralding the visitors as peacemakers because of what they did on the day of destruction. They are painting a beautiful picture of a future with them in charge."

David shook his head, "Yeah. Now that I am looking at this in a different light, I can see how this applies to our visitors. What or who do you think that they are if not aliens?"

"Well, remember the Book that Enikilo most clearly didn't like?" David shook his head yes. "There is a reason. It portrays the Ebgalians as the fallen angels that had sex with human women based on Genesis six. The giants mentioned in Genesis six were the Nephilim. I looked into Enoch and found that the book went into much detail about some of the names of the fallen angels and a detailed description of the Nephilim. If true, our visitors are nothing more than fallen angels that have been allowed to return to earth for a last day's deception."

"Second Thessalonians chapter two really is where I find that these visitors are deceivers. 'Brethren, concerning the coming of our Lord Jesus Christ and our meeting together with Him, we ask you, not to be easily shaken in mind or disturbed, either by spirit or by word or by letter, as if from us, that the Christ had come already. Let no one deceive you by any means; for that Day will not come unless the great falling away comes first, and the man of sin is exposed, the son of damnation, who opposes and exalts himself above all that is called God or that is worshiped, so that he sits as God in the temple of God, showing himself that he is God.' We have yet to see him sit at the temple, but he sure is setting himself up as at least equal to God, isn't he? He speaks of Enlil, who is Jehovah in the Old Testament, as just one of them- an alien that has been here all along. He is setting himself as opposing the God of the Bible and acting superior to Him."

David was quiet for the first time I have known him, "I will read on, 'And now you know what is restraining, that he may be exposed in his own time. For the mystery of lawlessness is already at work; only He who now restrains will do so until He is taken out of the way.' The 'aliens' that have been seen are nothing more than the fallen angels. They were restricted in what they can do because God Himself prevented them from exposing their deception. But now they have been cut loose."

David's eyes lit up as I was talking, "That is amazing! Why hadn't I seen this before? I sat under Doctor Card's teaching. I have heard these verses, but Doctor Card had put his twist on them, so I didn't have understanding of those verses. Please go on!"

"Going further in the same passage, 'Then the lawless one will be exposed, whom the Lord will devour with the breath of His mouth and destroy him with the brightness of His coming. The coming of the lawless one is similar to the working of Satan, with all power, signs, and lying wonders.' They have done some big things for mankind, showing their power, signs and wonders, haven't they?" Again, David silently shook his head.

"I'll read on in the same passage, 'and with all unrighteous trickery among those who perish, because they did not receive nor love of the truth, that they could be saved. And for this reason, God will send them strong delusion, that they should believe the lie, that they all may be condemned who did not believe the truth but had pleasure in unrighteousness.'"

"In other words, since humanity has rejected the true and living God, He has unleashed this 'great deception' into the world in preparation for the Second Coming. Here is how God described it to me within my heart and through scripture. God is separating his sheep from the goats. In this way, He is creating a dividing line to eliminate those who are sitting on the fence. He is doing it in a way that makes it clear who are His and who are not."

David shook my hand, "Rob, thank you for taking the time to share your research. It sure does make sense in light of what we have seen. You have connected what has happened to scripture and it makes sense. I gotta go for now. Gotta get ready if we need to leave town!"

David left. I felt good. Even though I am not an ordained minister, God used me to help someone today. I had a real good feeling inside.

Chapter 29 Statewide Crackdown

Governor John Craney did a live broadcast the next day, "Ladies and gentlemen, I come to you today concerning the matter that has been laid out before us. We have fully cooperated with our visitors in providing great incentives for you to get the Cure. We have firsthand seen the results of those who have come forward and performed their civil duty to take the Cure on a voluntary basis. It really is amazing to see the results of the Cure. I have asked some volunteers to come forward to interview with us today. The first one is Bobby. Come on up, Bobby!" An African-American lady stepped up to the governor and they greeted each other. "Bobby, can you tell us where you are from?"

She stepped up the microphone, "Hi. My name is Bobby."

Some from the crowd said, "Hi Bobby!"

She smiled and continued, "I am from Toledo, Ohio."

The governor asked, "Can you tell us about your background and how the Cure helped you?"

"I have suffered with chronic depression all my life. Many of family members have had this issue also. My mom, bless her soul, suffered from depression all of her life until she passed on about five years ago. I have had to take depression and anxiety pills since I was in seventh grade. The dosages had continually gone up and I have had to resort to stronger medication in the last four years. I took the Cure when it first came out. My doctor recommended it. Since I have had the Cure, there was a peace in my heart that I have had that I have never had before. I have been weaned off of the medications that I was on and now am depression FREE." She started to shout and wave her hands in the air out of gratitude and walked off the stage, crying in joy as she left. The audience applauded her.

The governor said as he applauded, "That is great Bobby! Jim, would you come forward?"

I thought Jim looked familiar, but I wasn't sure where I had seen him before. He stepped right up and started talking. "Hi, I'm Jim and I am an addict."

He paused. A few quietly responded with the typical AA response, "Hi Jim."

"Well, I have had addiction problems since I was 9 years old. It started with stealing my parent's vodka. I would drink some of the bottle, then filled it back up with water so they wouldn't know. I went from there to getting drugs from school faced a lot of time in jail as a result of my addiction. I turned to a life of crime and recently was found guilty of using a false ID to continue my addiction."

That was it! When I went to that convenience store after the meeting at Frank Fuller's house, I remembered the man with the severed thumb that he used for identification. That was his false ID he was talking about. "Instead of prison time, I was given the choice of taking the Cure. Since taking the Cure, I have not picked up nor drank. I don't even think about using. That struggle inside is over. When I start feeling anxious, I can feel the cure kick in and helping me through my feelings. I previously had to take meds for my anxiety. Now I don't have to do anything. The Cure truly is the cure for me. I am so grateful for what our visitors have done for me. I give them all the credit! I am indebted to them!" He looked into the camera directly and said, "Enikilo, if you all are listening, I personally thank you!" He then looked at the governor and the crowd, "Thank you for this opportunity and thank you for listening." He left the podium and applause could be heard from the crowd and from the governor.

"So, there you have it. This is just two of a vast number of people across the state that have found the "Cure" to be their cure. Mental problems, addiction issues, crime problems, improved methods for detecting and preventing medical problems. Many, many other issues have been cured by the Cure. We get to see two of the results today. I get to see many responses daily."

"With all of this going for the Cure, I ask, 'Why are you waiting?' We are stepping up our measures as suggested by Enikilo. In two weeks, it will be mandatory for all to take the Cure. In four weeks, we will have the security protocols set up. Until then, you have time to cooperate or you will not be able to get medical help, buy or sell anything. I wish that I didn't have to do this, but I am left with no choice."

"Those that are still uncured will be detained and will be sent to Cure camps to help them to understand our plight. Their refusal to cooperate is putting all of us in danger of going back to where we were just a few weeks ago, ready to annihilate each other and destroy this planet that we call home."

As I sat there listening to this speech, I felt like I was in a post-apocalyptic sci-fi movie where the evil empire is forcing cooperation. Worse yet, I was actually seeing the words of John come to life. I turned to Revelation thirteen and read these words, "He caused all, no matter who they were, to take a mark on their right hand or on their foreheads, and that no one may buy or sell unless they have the mark or the name of the beast, or the number of his name. Here is wisdom. Let him who has understanding calculate the number of the beast, for it is the number of a man: His number is 666."

A commercial for the Cure came on that shook me to the core...

"What is the Cure? Many have seen the number '666' as being correlated with "the mark of the Beast" in the antiquated Bible. Your friends, the visitors, encourage you that true safety and protection stems from ongoing personal empowerment and spiritual growth. Be open to the love and light brought to you by our good friends. Please understand that as you continue moving forward, a new light will shine into your light into your soul and you will then understand what real joy and peace is. Remember, your friends are here to support you on your personal spiritual path, but it does take a certain amount of courage, change, and awareness to step forward. You have the perfect opportunity for expansion and improvement to help you walk into your more perfect self. So, when you see the number '666', be comforted. It is the symbol of progress."

I need to talk to Frank. I haven't seen him in a while...

Chapter 30 A Visit to Frank's House

I parked at the 7-11 where I had parked at previously and went to Frank's house. I knocked on the door. I heard some scurrying around in the house and then I heard the distinct sound of a shotgun cocking. I assured him by saying, "Hey Frank, this is Rob. I just wanted to talk to you." The door opened a crack and I could see the end of a shotgun barrel pointing at me.

"Let me see your right hand." I pulled up my sleeve and displayed my hand, front and back. He opened up the door to let me in and shut the door behind me, securing it with deadbolt locks. "Sorry! I can't take any more chances. Jim outed me and several of our friends. You caught me just in time. I am getting ready to bug out.

"Jim? Jim Borkowski? I thought he had made a commitment to Jesus not too long ago! What happened?"

Frank got a sad look on his face, "Jim was arrested and they brainwashed him. They talked him into taking the mark. I guess once you take the mark, it completely changes you. He gladly spilled the beans about our operation. One of my covert friends is still on the force and saw it himself. He told about the plans that he knew about. He named me in particular and several others that were here that night, including you. You should make plans to leave town like I am. They will detain me for sure! They might do the same to you."

"What about your wife? Is she going with you?" I asked, "I am asking because I am thinking about my wife and kids. I could just take off, but what about them? I can't just leave them!"

Frank said, "She is coming too. She is afraid of what they might do to her too. She is still packing upstairs. She had not prepared for a day like this like I did. I am all ready. She still is putting things together. This is why I always had an EDC and a bug out bag so I could leave quickly. I guess I should have had her do the same, huh?" We quietly chuckled.

I said, "I wish I would have been better prepared. I don't even know if I can talk my wife into packing up and leaving, even on a short notice. She isn't really in on all that I have been involved in, mainly because I wasn't sure about her willingness to go along with all this. I guess we should get things together just in case. I will need to talk to her to get things ready at home. I have heard of bug out bags, but what is an EDC?"

"EDC is short for every day carry. It is a small bag of things I take with me every day to be ready for emergencies. It is also what I carry in my pockets. A knife, tools, other supplies that would make life easier to live in an emergency."

"Sounds like something that I need to do and do quickly. I am not sure what I might do. I have a place to go to if I decide to leave. However, I am definitely not ready to leave like you. I have no bug out bag, no EDC, and my wife is not aware of things like she should be. That's all my fault." I looked in earnest to Frank, "Where do I start, Frank?"

"I would start by talking to your wife. She needs to be on board with you and your plans. Next, I would throw together all your camping gear. Grab your essential clothes, medicines, toiletries and tools. Make sure you have a knife, hatchet, and shovel. You will need water, canned food or any other foods that are non-perishables. There are so many other things, but that's a good start." Sondra came down the stairs, a little frazzled. I could see by her countenance that she was not happy about what was going to happen. She looked up and saw me.

She was startled at first, not expecting to see anyone else in the house. She smiled then, realizing that I was not a threat, and greeted me.

"Sondra, it is good to see you!" I said, then, looking to both of them, "I guess we may not see each other any time soon. I know better than to ask where you are going. The less we know about each other's business, the better off we all are. Right?"

Frank shook his head, "Yes. It is wise to keep it all silent, because we never know who to trust. Jim is proof of this, isn't he?"

"Oh yeah! That's for sure! I am not sure who I can trust. David was all pro-visitors but woke up to the reality and now is refusing the 'Cure'. He will not take the Mark at any cost. Well, you are all ready and I don't want to delay you anymore. God bless you, my friend!"

"God speed, brother!" said Frank. We shook hands and left.

As I walked back to the car, I saw police cars speed by. I turned around and saw that they were pulling up to Frank's house. I stopped and prayed for their safe departure quickly and then moved on. My heart began to pump and I wondered if they had come to my house. I went home immediately.

Chapter 31 Visitors at Home

As I drove into the drive at my house, my worst fears were confirmed. An unmarked car was in front of our house and there were two men at my door that had guns and cuffs. There was Lisa, with a look of fear on her face as she was talking to them. I walked up to the house and asked, "How can I help you?"

The closest officer looked at me and asked, "Are you Robert Beck?"

"Yes, I am. How can I help you?"

We have been given intel that you might have been involved in an underground resistance movement. Do you know a Frank Fuller?"

"I have met him in a church and visited his house occasionally. Why? What has he done now?"

"As I said, he was involved in an underground visitor resistance movement and our source says you were seen at one of his meetings when he started the local resistance movement. Were you there?"

Well, I am not a good liar. Also, I am not one that believes lying is a good thing, so I told them the truth, "I was there one night to find out what it was all about. I like to research things before I make decisions of commitment."

"What did you think about it all?"

"Well, Frank is known for his conspiracy theories. He always has a bug out bag and an, (I pause, like I am thinking.) Each Day Carry... I think that is what it is called. At any rate, he didn't disappoint me about his conspiracy theories. He sure had a lineup of details about our visitors." As I was talking, I tried to smile and shake my head to give the impression I thought that Frank was a little different. "Don't get me wrong, I like the guy, but sometimes, he goes a little too far in his ideas."

"So did you get any signs from him to post up that contained anti-visitor information?"

"I did. Someone gave them to me, but I didn't do anything with them. I never asked for them. I didn't post them up or anything. In fact, let me try to find them. That way I can prove that I wasn't actually involved in the vandalism, right?"

The officer said, "I would love to see them. It would be helpful to you. Why didn't you bring them to the authorities though? That would have been the right thing to do."

"I didn't want to get anyone into trouble. Some of these people were friends and you know that there would be questions. Also, I thought they might be worth something as an antique a few decades from now. Let me go get them. Is that okay?" The officer shook his head yes and I walked into the house.

I dug out the folder of signs and brought them to the officer. "Here you go. You can keep them if you want. I didn't want to post them up anyway."

One of them took the flyers, looked at me, and said, "We checked our records. You and your family have not taken the Cure yet. Why is that?"

"As I had already said, I do like to investigate into things before I commit to them. The Cure was one of those issues that I have hesitated to commit to. The resistance was another issue that I checked out, but didn't commit to. I am responsible not only for myself, but my family too. So, if I err on the side of caution, can you blame me? I love my family!"

"You know you have less than two weeks to get the Cure. I would be taking care of this soon if I were you. We will be keeping track. Good day sir." He turned to Lisa, "Good day, ma'am."

Well, I dodged THAT bullet. As they left, I knew what was coming next. "Rob, what were you thinking? I told you to be careful! Now you put our whole family at risk? For what? Your curiosity? The kids are scared to death now! They thought they were going to lose their daddy!"

"Lisa, I know. It was exactly the way I said it was. I only went to Frank's that one night. I didn't realize it was going to take it this far. I'm sorry! I wouldn't have gone if I would have known that it would have gone this far. Let's go in and talk to the kids."

After hugging the children and talking to them, we prayed together as a family and they went to bed. Lisa and I had time to talk. "We have a big decision to make. Lisa, what do you think about the Cure?"

Lisa answered, "It sounds like they aren't giving us much choice if we want to live beyond the two weeks. What else can we do? I see nothing that will be a long-term solution. What do you think?"

"It seems like we can either take the Cure or we can go into a rural location and hide. I know a place where we could hang out for a while that would help us until we know more. What do you think about that option?"

"Rob, that doesn't seem like a long-term solution. It is also risky to reject the Cure. I don't want to be detained. If both of us are in detained, what will happen to the children. However, I am still not sure about this cure either."

"How about if we prepare for the worst-case scenario and prepare to leave for the country? We don't have to decide until the cutoff date, right?"

Lisa agreed, "That's true. We especially don't need to decide tonight. It is one of my night's off. I would like to get a good night's sleep. I'm still not happy that you put me in that situation tonight. I just want to let you know that you still aren't off the hook yet." We laughed and hugged.

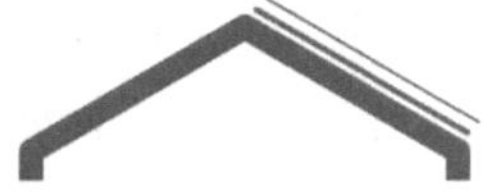

Chapter 32 The Beast Moves to Rome

A few days later, the typical interference came over the television again. However, the image of Enikilo was not what we saw. It was another Ebgalian. The right eye looked like it had been injured though. He smiled and said, "Greetings! I am Enmedigo. I am the one that was shot on the day our ship arrived to your "cradle of civilization". On that day, we were not on a military mission. However, today, we are preparing to take our rightful acts to lead you into your next evolutionary leap."

"As the leader of the Ebgalians, I proclaim to you that you should follow our simple instructions. Enikilo described to you the easy instructions. He has worked for centuries to formulate the Cure to supply the corrective measures for your DNA. I say again, just like I did the day I was shot, if we didn't care for you so much, we wouldn't have bothered with saving you from your Armageddon."

"In spite of our care for you and our investment in you over the millenniums, there are those among you that refuse to submit to our guidance. This is unfortunate. If enough people do not get the Cure, there is a risk of that dreadful sinful nature being brought back into your DNA. We cannot afford that risk. Neither can you. You must take the steps to ensure that every human submits to the Cure."

"The worst of the resisters are the Christians. They seem to be clinging to their scriptures and their traditions rather than believing what is in front of their eyes. They would rather believe the ramblings of John about the evils of 666 than to realize that 666 is a call to return to balance, to refocus, and to take your next step on your personal spiritual path for healing."

"It was their backward thinking that inspired that man to shot me on the day of our appearing. His attack on me killed me. However, the miraculous medical team on our ship brought me back to life after three days. I still suffer to this day with my obvious loss of sight in my right eye." He pulled back his long parka overshirt to reveal his right arm, which was shriveled. "I also have lost most of the use of my right arm."

"Today, we are moving to a more strategic location in preparation for the next steps we must take. We ARE your creators! We ARE your real 'gods'. We ARE the ones that breathed life into your forefathers. We ARE the ones that felt compelled to make you more like us. We ARE the ones that inspired your prophets to live better and resist your baser side. We ARE your 'saviors'. We ARE your 'messiahs'."

"We are moving to a place prepared for us, in the Vatican City. Saint Peter's square was built to accommodate our ship long ago. We prescribed the layout of the Vatican Square to Pope Alexander VII in 1664. From there, we can have not only the needed security, but also the ability to set up our rulership over the world."

"I again emphasize, we are not here to harm you. We are here to help you. Preparations are already underway to begin our move. This area has been cleared for our takeoff. We are moving. That's all for now."

The TV phased out. And the news media were ready to take over after Enmedigo's speech. The aerial cameras were fixed on the ship. The newscasters talked about the removal of everyone from the ship. Suddenly, the ship took off, not in a cloud of dust like any of our ships would. It just lifted off of the ground with, I presume, some kind of antigravity type power. The legs of the craft pulled up and the ship left so fast, it was as if it disappeared.

There were cameras all over at St Peter's Square. The ship appeared over the Square. The legs came back down and the ship landed in the

Square. The higher parts of the ship towered over the columns of the square, but the lower part of the ship fit perfectly within the Square. The front of the ship faced St Peter's Basilica, just like it was meant to be that way. Even the Obelisk in the middle of the square fit into the concaved center of the ship. The two fountains were unharmed also. It was, as Enmedigo said, "built to accommodate" the ship. The temporary walkways that were used to help visitors line up for various functions had been removed in preparation for the arrival of the ship.

The Vatican Guard came out, fully armed. They didn't face the ship, guarding everyone from those in the ship. They faced away from the ship, protecting the ship from everyone else. Enmedigo and several others that looked like security detail left the ship and walked directly into St Peter's Basilica, accompanied by security from both the Vatican and the Ebgalians.

The newscaster said that they were informed that it was a Ebgalian/Vatican summit. The details of the summit were unknown, but that more information would be forthcoming. Then a Vatican representative was being interviewed. He said that he is able to share facts that have been classified by the Vatican.

The Vatican have been in communication with the Ebgalians for a long time. The Vatican gave this statement, "As time has come closer to their revelation, we started to ready our followers. We previously gave statements to ready the public for this day. We shared that intelligent extraterrestrial life may exist on many different worlds, that they may not have experienced the Fall, and they could be baptized. It also was leaked long ago that there would be a war between those who befriend aliens and those who would not."

"These prophecies have come to complete fulfillment. There are those that are resisting the Cure. They have drawn a line, refusing it because of some misinterpreted ideas in Revelation. We are here to make it clear that the Pope gives his full support to the Cure and is telling his followers to participate in the plan. His statement will be forthcoming."

Chapter 33 The Two Witnesses

The next day, the news media broke in to reveal a striking event.

"Two people broke into the Vatican's St. Peters Square. Security attempted to stop them. As they did, these unarmed men shot something like fire at them, killing them. Let's break into the live feed as they are standing."

I could see two men, standing by the statues that were in front of the ship. The announcer said they were the Statues on the Façade in front of St Peter's Basilica.

They finally started broadcasting what the two people were saying. They said, "These people, who are called aliens or visitors are not aliens at all. They are actually fallen angels that have been kicked out of heaven and sent to this earth. They are here to do satan's bidding."

"They were the ones that caused Adam and Eve to sin in the garden! They were the ones that brought the curse upon the earth. They were the ones that put the sinful nature into the souls of man by tempting Eve to eat the fruit of the knowledge of good and evil!"

"They were the ones that corrupted your forefathers before the flood. They brought wickedness into the world, causing horrible losses of lives. They were the ones that had sex with the daughters of men and brought abominations into the world. It was their influence that caused God Almighty to grieve to the point of having to flood the earth to destroy the world."

"They had been under restrictions by God almighty so they could no longer interfere with humanity as they had done before the flood.

Only when the day of apocalypse came did God loosen the restrictions on these evil creatures to prevent disaster and to bring an end times deception upon us all."

"Enikilo is nothing more than the serpent, the devil, the accuser, satan... the dragon of Revelation 12. He is the that gives power to the beast who is the one called Enmedigo. They are the ones that have brought evil and corruption to this earth. They are furthering their corruption with this thing called the Cure. It is a poison straight from hell! Do not accept this vile corruption. Anyone who does will heap coals of fire on their own heads and seal their fate for eternity."

"Like the prophets of old, let us show you all a sign that we are from God Almighty and Jesus Christ His only begotten. We pray that the skies be dried up and that there would be no rain until we are taken up into heaven." At that point every cloud in the sky evaporated at the Vatican. It was raining outside at home at this time also. I heard the rain stop and the sun came out and the birds began to chirp.

The other man spoke up, "My friend is correct. These Ebgalians are merely angels that started in heaven. They followed Lucifer in his fall, so they were rejected by Almighty God. They were in heaven, experiencing every blessing. They were in the very Presence of God and experienced His glory. They rejected the Great and Mighty Lord and were cast out of heaven."

"Since they were rejected by God, hatred filled their hearts. They wanted to get back at the Most High God. They discovered humanity and found out that God had a love for us. Therefore, since they wanted to exact revenge, they did all they could to get back at the Lord by manipulating His creation."

"They invented false religions, starting with the Sumerian tablets. They set themselves up as gods and lowered the Mighty One in Heaven in their fables to just another one of them. They still had to admit in the tablets that the one they called Enlil (who is Almighty God) was the greatest of all. I tell you that He is the one and only God.

These imposters passed themselves off as gods in the past. They are now passing themselves off as visitors from another planet."

"Here is a word from the Lord. Jesus proved who He was by laying in the grave for 3 days, but then He arose! Enmedigo copied this in his death for three days. Strike down these bodies and they will arise again within 4 days. When God brings us back from the dead, it will be a witness against these foul creatures."

From behind them, as they were continuing their speech, Enmedigo appeared with a weapon. The look on his face was one of complete hatred, he looked at both of them and fired his weapon quickly. They were struck in the heart and fell forward into the Vatican Square.

Enmedigo proclaimed, "Let them lay where they fell. They died just like any man will die. Their bodies will rot in front of you. Keep your cameras on them for four days to show they are merely human beings. I died and was brought back to life. They will not be that fortunate. They were unappreciative of our gracious gifts which we freely gave to all of humanity."

"This will be a sign to you that this archaic Christian faith that only honors Enlil and rejects the rest of us. This outdated religion was brought down from a cursed people, the Israelites. I am proclaiming to you that these two men represent EVERYTHING that is wrong with this world. Those who hold to this faith, are my enemies. They should be your enemy too. Every government is, from this point, to make proclamations against the Christian faith. The actions of these two have forced my hand. Now I command the world to bow before my presence or be obliterated, just like these two fools!"

I could feel the chills going up and down my spine. Frank was right! I should have left long ago. Is Lisa ready for this? I sure wish I would have confided in her a month ago. Everything happened so fast!

Chapter 34 "I Need to Get Out of Here!"

As you might imagine, David came to the door within 15 minutes. As he came in, he said "Wow! Can you believe what that... demon, fallen angel, antichrist... Whatever you want to call it! He wants the world to bow to him! He wants us to cave in to his demands! He wants us to worship him. Well, I will never cave in to him. I need to get out of here. The police know that I have not taken the cure. They know that Harriet hasn't taken it too. They stopped in the other day, asking about you and checked on our status. Harriett and I are leaving as soon as we can get all our stuff around. Fortunately, I have kept a stock of medicine and rotated them so I have at least a four-month supply. Are you coming with us?"

Lisa came into the room to see what the clatter was. "Oh, hi David! I was worried that it was the police or something. We were warned the other day about getting the vaccine and with what I saw on the TV, I was concerned that they might have come here already."

"Lisa," I said, looking at her, "We need to talk." I looked at David and said, "I will get back with you soon. I have to get some things together with Lisa."

David looked down and said, "I understand. Prayers for you, my friend." He left immediately.

"First, what is your opinion at this point about the Cure now?"

"They ARE making it mandatory. I not only am thinking about myself, but for our children. They need to go to school, if we do not go along and get the Cure, we will be detained. If we run, they will eventually catch up with us and we would lose the children. I couldn't handle it if that happens. They are my life. If we both lose them, there will be nobody to raise them. I plan on cooperating with the plan and take the Cure. Even if you don't take the Cure, I will. I will not tell you what to do. However, if you don't take the cure, you will need to leave. We just can't take the chance of you putting the rest of us in danger. These visitors are powerful and the State of Ohio is following along with the visitors."

I blame myself. I should have talked to Lisa a long time ago. Now she has come up with an answer based on her biggest personal need. Security. All I can do is share with her what I know about how these "visitors" have fulfilled every prophecy about the end times and the antichrist. I tried to give her all the various details.

"Lisa, they demand that we worship him. We must take a mark on our hand or forehead in order to buy and sell. Dr Card predicted that the antichrist would set up at the Vatican. The 'beast' came out of the sea just like it said in Revelation. Did you hear those two men on the television just now? They said that these visitors are fallen angels and the source of all of our problems. Those two men at the Vatican were the two witnesses spoken of in Revelation. They will be raised again within 4 days! If they do raise from the dead, would you reconsider? Can you put off taking the Cure at least until then."

It was like I was talking a foreign language to her. She had made up her mind and I was not going to change it. Lisa would not even look up to me. I repeated to her, "Could you at least wait to take the Cure until those four days are complete. If those two witnesses rise from the dead, then you will have the proof you need. If they are still rotting on the fifth day, you will know that I was wrong. After they raise, you will have your proof that I am right and you shouldn't take the Cure. You can email me then. Do we have a deal?"

She was still silent, standing there with her eyes closed. I continued, "I can't choose to take the mark, which is what the Cure is. I am sure of it. I will be leaving with David shortly." I called David and told him to wait for me and I packed for the trip to the farm. I told him that I would be coming alone.

"Lisa, I love you, and would love for you all to come with me, and the Cure is not what it seems. Are you sure?" Still the silent treatment. "Do I get a kiss?" She started to cry and shook her head no. "OK. If things clear up, I will check back with you. Goodbye." I left for David's house and went to the farm, crying all the way.

Chapter 35 Bill's Hideout

We arrived at Bill's house. The dogs were barking as we rolled into the drive. Bill came out to greet us. "Hey! How's it going?"

David shook Bill's hand, "Well, we made it here. We figured we had better get out here before the hammer comes down. Things are getting quite difficult in town." David turned to me, "You know Rob."

Bill said, "Yep. I guess you didn't get that '71 Monte Carlo, huh?"

We all laughed, "Nope. She wouldn't spring for it. But she also wouldn't join me in coming out here. I wasn't telling her all the details about all the signs that I saw until today. She wanted to be secure. She was afraid that she would lose the kids. She may change her mind, but I don't want to bring her out here unless I know that she really has had a change of heart. I don't want to risk everyone's life because I want my wife. So how do you keep updated on what is happening? Do you have a television?"

As we walked into the house, Bill answered, "Oh yeah! I have an antenna to watch the news. It's been quite the drama, huh?" He walked over to the TV.

David said, "Oh yes! I am seeing prophecy being fulfilled almost every day. What's on now?"

Bill answered, "They are showing those two guys rotting in the Pope's Square by that ship. Rather boring if you ask me. Who cares that their bodies are laying there? I am just glad that I ain't there. Can you imagine that smell after a few days?"

David explained, "These two guys are in Revelation. The Bible says that they will come back to life after three and a half days and be taken up to heaven. It will prove that the Living God, the God of the Bible is greater than those fallen angels that are trying to take control of the world. You really should reconsider your beliefs. I will be more than glad to help you to understand what is happening according to the Bible..."

Bill started to laugh, "Look man, if these guys do come back from the dead, I will be more than glad to listen to you. I really don't have time for such fables."

"Do I have your word, Bill?" David said, "I will take you up on that. If these two guys rise from the dead, I will share with you not only the prophecies that both Rob and I see being fulfilled, but I will talk to you about the One that died about 2000 years ago and came back to life." They shook hands.

"Deal. You can tell me about God and I will teach you about survival. For now, though, we need to take care of more practical things. You need to unload everything out of the car and park the car in the old shed so nobody knows you are here."

We unloaded the car and hid it in the shed. We got our property moved into the old bedrooms upstairs. I looked around my room. It had some REALLY old green wallpaper with flowers and vines. I had to laugh at the thought that someone had a believed that that wallpaper was attractive.

Bill showed us around the house. He showed us the stash of food he had in the basement, the kitchen, his gas heater and stove that requires no electricity, which is fed by his own natural gas well, and other various preparations for this day.

He was a prepper, for sure! I am grateful that he was one today. Just a few months ago, I would have thought he was a little off his rocker. I never cared for how wild these guys could be. I watched YouTube videos of all their preparations for emergencies and laugh at the crazy plans they had. I am not laughing now. I just hope for the chance for David and I to witness to him so he is prepared for eternity.

Chapter 36 The Two Witnesses are Risen

It is hard to believe how fast three days can go by, but I had been focused on learning how to start fires, making rocket stoves out of large metal cans and bricks, and some other survival skills that just might come in handy sometime in the future. Bill has been training for this type of situation for quite some time and seems happy to share his knowledge, as well as some of his extra supplies to help me. Who knows when I might need these skills?

We worked on escape plans if the sheriff stops in to check on us. We set up David's car as the getaway vehicle. Our "bug out" equipment is in the shed near David's car, ready to be loaded in case we need to drive off quickly. He told us that he had a fallout shelter in case of a nuclear disaster, but he refused to disclose its location.

We turned on the television to see the latest events. Even when they are talking about other events around the world, there is a window at the bottom right side, showing the dead bodies of the two witnesses. By now, there are flies gathering and those who come to see the decaying bodies are wearing masks and reacting to the smell of the corpses.

This was the big day. It was the day when the two witnesses were to arise, if they were truly the two witnesses. I have staked a lot of my hopes that they were. Over the last three days, I have been thinking things like, "What if they were just some deranged men, like the gunman on the day the beast came out of the sea." Those doubts crept in occasionally and I had to drive them out. My future with Lisa and the kids are at stake. David also had a deal with Bill. If these two guys were just common men, would he ever believe?

So, we are all sitting around the living room, listening to the latest news about the Cure, about the resistance, and about the so-called visitors. In one corner of the screen, a view of the two witnesses was placed. Every once in a while, they would put the bodies on the main screen, showing that they are still dead. The newscasters regularly would sneer at the television while reporting on anything that opposes Enmedigo and Enikilo, but especially when they talked about the two witnesses.

Evidently, someone did their homework, because the news media also were aware of the three-and-a-half-day prophecy in Revelation eleven because when it was closer to that hour, they began to show the bodies with everything else on the small image. They told about the background of the two and interviewed with people that knew them. They, of course, interviewed only those with the Cure and had nothing good to say about the two witnesses. While these people looked normal, when they talked, it was as if they had been brainwashed. They spoke of their love for Enmedigo and Enikilo and their disdain for the two guys. Every time they did, Bill had to talk back to them, holding a beer in his hand and spilling a little beer out when he got really excited.

My doubts weren't helped by the hatred expressed and the criminal records of the witnesses. They didn't have a flowery background. One had a record a mile long with drug charges and forgery. It sounded like it was from a while ago, so my hope is that they made a commitment to Jesus since then. I kept telling myself that Jesus saves the worst of us and God had delivered him. The Savior many times uses the worst of us to do the biggest jobs. Bill would look at me when they talked of his past and shake his head and say things like, "It doesn't sound good for your so-called 'witnesses'. My friend. He was no saint". I kept telling him that we don't have the full story. He would admit, "Well, that's true. I am the first to know that we can't trust the media."

The cameras, that were resting on the ground, started to shake from the ground trembling. Bill, as well as the rest of us, leaned forward, staring at the screen. The bodies moved, sat up, and soon were in an upright position. One of them looked into the camera, saying, "We told you that God Almighty would bring us back to life. This is all the proof you need that these charlatans that you call 'The Visitors' are no gods. They are the antichrists spoken of in the Word of God. They are nothing more than the fallen angels that deceived Eve in the Garden of Eden, they are the ones that tempted Jesus in the desert, they are the ones that entered Judas, they are the ones that accuse the brethren. They are called by many names, including the prince and power of the air, the serpent, the dragon and his false prophet."

"Repent from your sins! Follow the Lord and Savior Jesus Christ, the Son of God, and His teachings found in the Bible!"

Bill dropped his beer on the floor. He didn't even try to pick up the mess. He looked at me and said, "I am ready now."

"We are going to pray. Now if you mean this prayer with all your heart, God will hear your prayer and will give you His Holy Spirit as a witness. If you don't experience it now, seek Him until you find him. OK?" Bill stared at me and shook his head yes. I said, "Let's pray. Repeat after me."

"I believe that Jesus Christ, the Son of God came to earth to save me, and that by His death on the Cross, He paid the price for my sins, so that I might have everlasting life. Thank You this free gift of salvation. Thank You for the forgiveness of my sins. Thank You, Lord, for sending Your Son to die on Calvary's cross in my place."

"Lord, I turn from all my prideful sins and from everything that is dishonoring to You, and pray that I would grow in the grace and in a knowledge of Jesus. Transform my lowly life into the likeness of Jesus through the Holy Spirit. Thank You, Father, for Your gift of salvation and thank You that by believing I am now Your child. In Jesus' name I pray, Amen."

Bill, looking up to me with tears I have never seen before in him, said, "Thank you. I believe that God sent you to me for this moment. I feel His presence! I feel clean! I feel free!" We all praised God.

David, who never took his eyes of the television as we were praying and praising God, said, "Look at the TV!". The two witnesses had stopped talking. There was a thundering voice that said, "Come up here." There was a great earthquake and the two witnesses looked up and were taken up into the sky. There were drones overhead the Vatican and they caught the action of the upward path of the two witnesses.

Chapter 37 The Aftermath

While we were looking through the aerial drone cameras on the television, the great earthquake overtook the Vatican and portions of the city were destroyed. The Vatican developed a fissure through the center of city. The fissure ran through the Vatican Square and caused the square to be uneven. The back part of the ship was visibly lower than the front.

Cameras on the street demonstrated quite a variety of reactions. Some were simply frightened and attempted to run for cover. Others were praising God and giving Him glory in spite of all that was happening around them. They were lifting up their hands to heaven and glorifying God.

Others were panicked, having taken the Cure and realizing what they had done. While on the camera, some tried to remove the Cure. Some used knives while others, just attempted to remove the chip with their bare hands. They all ended up dying in their futile attempts.

I checked my email, hoping to hear word from home. Lisa had left me an email. She had not taken the Cure and knows the truth due to the two witnesses coming back from the dead. She asked if I would pick her and the kids up and that they were packed and ready to go.

David, my wife has asked me to pick her up. Can I borrow the car? She says she is ready to go. I just want to drive into town, pick them up, and bring them here."

David, of course, said, "Sure. Do you want me to go with you?"

"David, I would love it, but I don't want you to risk your life for me. Bill, do you mind if I bring them here? I really want my family here."

Bill smiled and said, "Can she cook? Oh, that's right. We have Harriot." He paused and laughed, "Of course you can! Do it soon before anything else can happen."

I got the keys, and got the car out of the shed and left for town. I made sure that I kept under the speed limit even though I wanted to speed. I couldn't wait to see Lisa and the kids!

At the house, I parked in back and went in the back door. Lisa saw me and we embraced. She stopped and said, "I am sorry that I didn't have faith in your judgement. I should..."

I interrupted her as I fondled her hair, "Look, we can talk later. We need to get out of town as soon as possible before anything else happens. Let's go!"

I greeted the kids, we gathered the stuff they had gotten together and packed them in the car. We started driving back to the farm when Lisa said, "Rob, I think we are being followed." I turned left down a county road, then turned left again. If someone was actually following us, they will continue following us. If they just happened to be going the same way we are, they would stop following us and go on their merry way. They were still behind us after two turns. I drove back into Findlay, and started making random turns in the streets to hopefully loose them. I was successful and started driving out of town again. We got back to the farm and hid the car in the shed. We stayed inside the shed for a few minutes just trying to collect ourselves before going in. I began to tell them a little of what happened over the last few days. While in the shed, we heard a helicopter and cars driving by. They might have been looking for us. I was glad we hid the car first and didn't leave the shed right away. Once it quieted down outside, we grabbed a handful of stuff and quickly went into the house.

Bill greeted us with, "What did you do to attract such a crowd? They were definitely looking for you." I explained to him what happened. He said that we did the right thing and was glad we took the precautions that we did. "Well, that's the last trip to town in a while!" Bill looked at Lisa, "I take it you are Lisa?"

Lisa said, "Yes I am. And you are Bill? On the way here, Rob told me of your generosity and hospitality. Thank you so much! It's my fault that Rob had to go into town to get us. I just didn't understand what was happening. When I saw those two witnesses rise from the dead, I knew that Rob was right."

Bill said, "David had the same deal with me and I just committed my life to Jesus Christ! Rob, you had a lot at stake with those two witnesses."

I said, "Oh yes I did! I was sweating it over the last few days, hoping that I was right." We laughed.

David and Harriet came into the room, David said, "Lisa, it is so good to see you and the children! I am glad you waited before taking the Mark. If you would have taken that mark of the Beast, you know what would have happened. I was praying for you every day! Harriet, being the good cook she is, made a special treat for everyone. Let's go in and enjoy!"

The kids were excited to get another one of Harriet's treats. She treated the kids often at home. I am glad she is here, especially due to her cooking skills. We all sat around the large dining room table, laughing and joking with each other. We shared scriptures, praises, and burdens. I am so glad that God sent Bill our way. He provided a safe shelter, at least for now. I know that it won't last forever, but we can enjoy this moment for now. It could all go away in a day. "One day at a time" is a paraphrase of what Jesus said, telling us not to worry about tomorrow.

For now, I have my wife, my family, two of my greatest long-term friends in David and Harriet, and a new friend, Bill. He has provided us with survival training, food, and all the comforts of home. Most of all, I am thankful for my Heavenly Father. He has cared for me even before

I knew Him. His Son, Jesus Christ, laid down His life for me so I could have eternal life. Even if I were to die tomorrow, I will spend the rest of eternity with God! That is the greatest security of all. I thank God for all of this.

Chapter 38 The President's Speech/ Enmedigo's Response

The next day, it was announced that President Pence was going to give an important speech at eleven a.m. So, I did the daily morning chores of feeding the animals and enjoying another one of Harriet's breakfasts. Then we did some cleaning and played with the kids. Lisa found that the house REALLY needed cleaning. I guess she found her purpose in our new little "commune." A little before the speech was to start, we sat down in the living room.

The news media was abuzz as to what President Pence was going to talk about. There were no leaks to the media like they normally did to prepare the us for what was coming up. Right at eleven, the cameras in the oval office were turned on and President Pence was sitting at his desk.

He shuffled his papers and look earnestly at the camera, "Good morning. The last few months have not been easy for anyone. It especially has not been easy for anyone to lead a country. I have been weighing each decision before making them and have held back on some decisions, weighing the consequences."

He shifted in his chair and said, "I have held off on a particular decision that cannot be delayed any longer. Recent events have forced my hand. It is about the Cure. I have allowed the states to make their decisions on it, keeping myself at a distance. Now is the time for me to take a stand."

"Our visitors have drawn a line in the sand, making the Cure mandatory in just a few days if one wants to buy or sell anything. This has always bothered me personally. You see, we are a country based on freedom. Over the last few decades, I have watched our freedoms slowly ebb away. But recently, our freedoms are being challenged and I have watched our states quickly taking away our precious freedoms."

"After the events of the last few days, I can no longer allow this to happen in our country. Making the Cure mandatory is unacceptable. Today, I am signing an executive order to revoke any state laws making the Cure mandatory. It is the only choice I can live with."

Bill put his hand in the air and shouted "YES!!!! That's my man!"

"As your president and as a man of faith, I am concerned about the results of the Cure. It is relatively untested by our scientists. I also have heard the words of the two witnesses before they were taken up to Heaven. Their coming back to life is proof enough for me to believe what they say."

"God bless you all and God bless America."

The media went berserk over the speech. Bill turned down the volume and said, "I don't need to hear them. We have seen how they have been on the wrong side of things." We talked about the possibility of a lifting of the state restrictions and that living a "normal" life might be possible.

As we were talking, Bill noticed that Enmedigo was on the TV, so he turned up the volume.

"It is unfortunate that the president of the United States has chosen to defy our mandates. This is a sad day for us because we had hoped this would go more smoothly. We must take swift action due to the insurrection. In the United States, our hand of protection will be removed. Train your cameras on the locations where the bombs were going to land. We spared you all from destruction, but we will no longer be able to spare the United States from their obliteration. In five minutes, watch America's annihilation."

"As was explained before, we have the ability to cause objects to appear and disappear into other realms. The missiles have been rocketing through empty space up to this time. In less than five minutes, they will be brought back to where they disappeared. This means they will hit their intended targets in America."

"Oh, no! The crap is going to hit the fan! Get ready to follow me. We will only have a few minutes to react."

The media placed their cameras into the air where the missiles disappeared and put the broadcast on a multiple screen broadcast. The news people are shouting about how the president is to be blamed. They also were telling how thousands were attempting to evacuate the cities and looting was taking place in the cities.

Suddenly, the missiles appeared out of a circle just like they disappeared. David exclaimed, "Oh dear Jesus, come quickly!" Harriet started to cry. Lisa had her arms around me and started to squeeze me tightly. One by one, the missiles landed and the cameras quit broadcasting.

Bill said, "Now is the time. Get the kids and come downstairs into the shelter. We won't have long." Lisa and I grabbed the kids and we all rushed to the basement. Bill shut the door. A rumble started and increased. The blasts from the bombs were arriving. The lights went out. Soon the sound was deafening. Destruction had come to America.